Curse of the Witch

David R. Smith

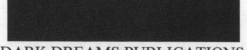

DARK DREAMS PUBLICATIONS

Copyright © 2020 by David R. Smith
All rights reserved. No part of this book may be reproduced without permission from the author, David R. Smith, 15 East Ave., Livonia, NY 14487, excepting for brief passages appearing in a review for a newspaper or magazine.

ISBN: 9780578632285

For ordering information, contact the author at

drs32@rochester.rr.com or visit

www.davidrsmithbooks.com

Printed in the United States of America

For my mother,
missing you every day

"And mark this. Let either of you breathe a word, or the edge of a word, about the other things, and I will come to you in the black of some terrible night and I will bring a pointy reckoning that will shudder you. And you know that I can do it."

Abigail Williams
-*The Crucible,* Arthur Miller

Curse of
the Witch

One night the rain began to fall...

...and the old man knew his time had come.

Not through any magical spells or sorcery, boiling cauldrons or crystal balls. It was a feeling of something amiss, a signal from some strange and dark place. His name whispered over and over, by an evil as ancient as time itself.

Spikes of fear stabbed the old man's heart. He was certain who was calling his name, who was coming for him tonight. He knew the legends and was a part of them himself.

She had come back.

The one who cursed him long before he was even born.

The old man's fingers trembled as he closed the grimoire he'd been browsing. A storm had kicked up out of nowhere, causing the power to fail. He was forced to read the book of spells by candlelight. The slithery movements of shadows caught his eye, the way they climbed and leapt from wall to ceiling in his bedroom. Every corner of the room quivered with them. The notion of a bottomless pit filled with vipers came to mind.

Shuddering violently, he found he couldn't breathe. His tongue sat like a hard lump on the bottom of his cottony mouth. He clutched at his chest and muttered an incantation under his breath, all the while trying unsuccessfully to push back the rising tide of horror inside him.

He hadn't the power to combat this dark magic, at least not alone. He was a dead man for sure.

The storm howled outside his cabin with the fury of demons. It beat its fists against the groaning walls. It screamed through the eaves. Then, suddenly, he heard the explosive shattering of glass. Violent wind raced through the cabin, ransacking everything in its path.

The old man stood on shaky legs and peered out the window at the fitful night. A burst of lightning cracked the sky and deafening thunder followed. *There's something very wrong about this storm*, he thought. And about the darkness itself. Something so sinister it could only be one thing, a magic far blacker than any he'd encountered before. But what power could unleash such frightful enchantment?

He started sifting through his books, looking for a possible explanation, when a strange smell filled the cabin. A sickly sweetness that reminded him of dying roses and rotten fruit.

Then, a sound followed the scent, a noise much closer and more distinct than the whispering of his name. A noise that made his heart lurch painfully and his throat dry up. A scratching-chafing-scraping sound coming from inside his own house.

From the other side of the door, where things were moving.

The old man moved to the door quickly and locked it. Then, scanning the room, he searched for a way to leave a message for the others when they arrived. A message that would not be discovered by the things outside when they broke down the door and dragged him away kicking and screaming into the night.

A chorus of howls from inside his own cabin froze his blood.

Panicked, he returned to the small writing desk in the corner where he'd been sitting and rifled through its drawers until he found a black pen. Then he hurried around the bed to the opposite wall. He removed a framed painting and set it on the bed face down. With shaky fingers, he started writing his secret message, a simple yet clever code for a certain child he had in mind, one who was exceptionally perceptive at seeing things as they truly were.

He hoped she'd get the message in time.

He hoped the *other* one wouldn't find it first because if the other one did, it would be all over. Not only would he be killed—a fate sure to be slow and painful—but a centuries-old pact would be broken. He'd have betrayed his ancestors' trust and unleashed a terrible and ancient evil upon the world.

From the door came the sounds of scratching, clawing, and cracking wood. Whatever was out there was only moments away from getting inside.

The old man finished his message and returned the painting to the wall. He dropped to his knees and closed his eyes.

He hoped it would be over soon.

Part
One

It is the essence of power that it accrues to those
with the ability to determine the nature of the real."

Arthur Miller, *The Crucible*

Chapter 1

"I DARE YOU TO jump," Ryan said, nudging his sister. "I don't want to swim all alone."

The glistening pool lay waiting for them to make their decision. Were they going to dive in or not? Ryan wanted his sister to do something other than sit by herself and read all day, but Abby was having none of it. She stood beside him like a statue, arms folded across her chest, her puckered face determined not to smile or have any fun at all.

She is so different, he thought for the millionth time, beginning with the day she came home from the

1

hospital. Unlike normal babies, she didn't cry or fuss. She was content to lay in her crib and stare oddly at the ceiling. Sometimes a funny expression flickered across her scrunched little face. In those moments she would often make a gurgling sound, wave, and then grow silent again. Ryan often wondered what she saw up there.

As she grew, Abby spent more and more time alone. She learned to read by age three. She talked in riddles and loved solving puzzles. She even invented a written alphabet that looked like ancient runes, whose meaning she never shared with anyone.

But perhaps the strangest thing about Abby was her fascination with the supernatural.

"If you don't go in, I'll push you," he warned. He placed a hand on her back, applied a little pressure. "You don't need to worry. You'll float like a feather; you always do."

That was another strange quirk about his sister. Water rejected her. If she tried to swim under it, water pushed her back up like it didn't want anything to do with her. He'd never seen anyone so buoyant before.

"Suit yourself," he said with a big sigh. "I'm going in. The sun is scorching my back."

Ryan cannonballed into the water, enjoying himself despite the sour look his sister was giving him.

"Hey, I'll give you ten dollars if you join me," he said when he emerged, pretending to take money out of his pocket. "No, make it *fifty*. Fifty dollars, and all you have to do is jump in. I'll be right here to save you if you start drowning, which you won't. They didn't name me captain of the varsity swim team for nothing, you know!"

Abby shook her head slightly. *You silly boy,* her expression seemed to say. *When will you ever learn?*

Ryan couldn't figure out what made his ten-year-old sister tick. Their parents thought it was autism; however, the specialist they'd consulted said that although she had some of the characteristics of autism, she was simply Abigail Rebecca Martin, blond-haired, green-eyed, pale-skinned, a shade under five feet tall, and quirky.

Very quirky.

Who else eats the food on their plate in alphabetical order? Or organizes the books in their bedroom by the Dewey Decimal System? She even taught Ryan who Melvil Dewey was, a librarian who came up with the classification system back in 1876.

A light breeze rippled the pool's surface. Abby looked up with curious intensity at the golden sunlight pouring down from the sky.

Anyone else would have jumped at the chance to make fifty bucks. But not his sister. Although she was strange, he had to admit he enjoyed her company. Like most people who talked very little, Abby was a good listener.

But the truth was she *did* speak, occasionally, though she didn't believe in wasting words on meaningless chatter. Like a host of one of those creepy paranormal shows, Abby would suddenly show up in his bedroom and start telling him about an ancient civilization or a mythological creature. He hung on every word; he couldn't help it. The oddities that tumbled out of her mouth were both bizarre and fascinating.

When she was finished, she would simply turn away from him and walk out. She didn't care if he had questions. He called those quirky moments *Abby Snapchats* because he didn't know what else to call them. They were random and intriguing, and although he'd admit it only to himself, those moments made him feel connected to his sister. He knew his relationship with her was not like other people's, but he didn't care. He was fond of Abby and felt highly protective of her.

"Let me see if I have this straight," he teased as he climbed out of the pool and walked over to the diving board. "You put on your bathing suit for nothing?"

She shrugged. "Mom made me." The words, like her expression, were curiously distant and detached.

The voice of someone waking from a dream.

"Well, suit yourself, Abs."

He drew in a deep breath through his nose. Then, tensing his legs, he sprang into the air, and sliced cleanly down through the water. His fingertips brushed along the smooth bottom of the pool. He kicked his strong swimmer's legs twice and glided through the cool water to the other side of the pool.

In that moment of bliss, he thought if there were such things as mermaids, he could swim with them forever. Of course, the only person he knew who believed in mermaids was Abby, who never met a superstition she didn't like.

When he surfaced, he shook the water out of his eyes and looked around.

Abby was gone.

In the few seconds he'd been underwater, she'd somehow managed to make her escape. He spied her in the screened-in back porch, legs tucked up under herself and a big fat book laying open in her lap.

Of course. What else would she be doing?

Okay, enough is enough, he thought. He was going to get her outside again one way or another, even if it meant tying a rope around her legs and dragging her kicking and screaming into the sunshine.

It was for her own good.

He toweled off and joined her on the porch. He couldn't see the cover of the book she was reading, but the title in the top margin read: *A Supernatural History of the World.*

"How can you sit there reading this depressing junk when it's a beautiful day outside?" he scolded her.

He waited for a response, but when all he got was the silent treatment, he decided it was time to take direct action.

"Abby," he said, flopping down on the couch next to her, "do you care that you're the only kid in the whole town not playing outside right now?"

"They should be reading, too."

The absurdity of her answer made him laugh. And

7

he knew she wasn't kidding. Abby was happiest when she was indulging her brilliant yet baffling mind in arcane subjects. Like their father, a former social studies teacher-turned-author who wrote books on ancient legends and folktales, Abby had a fondness for history. Especially dark history. And most amazing of all, her mind was a vacuum for knowledge. Nothing that went in ever came out. A photographic memory, Dad called it. A real blessing.

Or a curse, Ryan thought, depending on which way you looked at it.

Watching the intensity with which Abby was reading the book, he couldn't help wondering what was haunting that mysterious mind of hers today.

"I'm not leaving until you put that stupid book down and come outside," he declared.

"You'll have a long wait," she replied, casually turning a page.

"Okay, then." He snatched the book from her hands before she could protest. "I'm out of ideas; I guess I'll just harass you."

Abby gave a little yip like a wounded puppy. "Give it back, Ryan!"

"Hey, you're my kid sister, right? I gotta know what you're reading." He flipped through the pages and stared at the old, grainy illustrations. Here was the portrait of a man who looked to be at least a hundred years old, scowling fiercely in a long white wig. On the opposite page was an artist's sketch of an old-fashioned courthouse. A sobbing woman stood before an angry crowd of onlookers. She looked desperate and terrified as the panel of judges pointed at her accusingly. Ryan started reading aloud the caption below the photograph.

"'In 1694, Sara Gooding was charged with witchcraft and sentenced to death by hanging in Salem, Massachusetts. James Hathorne, one of the judges at her trial, later wrote in his personal diaries...'"

"'...that he felt regret for his role in the unjust murders of so many people,'" Abby interrupted. She recited the rest of the caption from memory: "'To this day, visitors to Salem hear screams in the middle of the night, and feel an unmistakable presence watching them. Are they imagining unseen spirits? Or are they experiencing the ghosts of Salem's haunted past?'"

Ryan gawped at his sister. It gave him a cold tingle whenever he witnessed Abby's amazing abilities. He couldn't seem to remember where he put his homework most of the time, and yet Abby could perfectly recite whole passages out of a book.

Without a word, he handed the book back to her and stood up.

"Okay, Abs, let's change the subject," he said, wringing his hands. "Wanna play Frisbee?"

"No."

"Ride bikes?"

"No."

"Why not?"

"It's going to rain," she said.

"*What?* There's not a cloud in the sky!"

10

"It's going to rain," she repeated flatly, keeping her attention on the book. Her lips moved slightly when she read, but she didn't utter a sound. He wondered if that was her trick to remembering all the words she read.

"I think you're crazy," he said.

"I'll exercise when I get to Uncle Silas's place tomorrow."

They were planning to spend a week with their mom's uncle in his cabin deep in the Adirondack mountains. They hadn't visited him in two years, and everybody, including Abby, was excited for the trip.

"Then what do you want to do instead now?" he asked.

She looked up at him. The answer was obvious.

"Fine." He was about to leave when an unusual anger welled up inside of him. He rarely felt anything but affection for his sister, but sometimes her inscrutable nature got under his skin.

"You know what your problem is?" he began.

11

"You're missing out on life. Yeah, you're smart, but books can't make up for the excitement of living and having fun."

He started to pace now, like their father did when he was lecturing them.

"Life isn't in those books, you know. You should get out more, make some friends. You fill your head with too much weird stuff. That's what's wrong with you—you don't believe in anything real!"

Outside, the sun slipped behind a cloud like a magician pocketing a coin.

"Then you know what your problem is, Ryan?" she answered him, closing the book with a loud thump. "You don't believe in anything you can't see or touch. You have no *faith*."

He froze. Her words stabbed him like daggers, but they didn't stop him from asking the question that was really on his mind. "What's wrong with you today, Abs? You're acting funnier than usual, even for you."

"Nothing."

"You're lying."

Abby chewed her lower lip, a nervous habit. When she spoke again, her voice contained a faint tremor. "It isn't lying if you don't want to tell the truth," she said.

"You know, you'd make a great politician."

Abby didn't respond to that, and he didn't push her anymore. Instead, he left the patio and was on his way back to the pool when he felt a drop of water strike his forehead.

He looked up.

The blue sky and the sun were gone.

It was starting to rain.

Chapter 2

THE AFTERNOON STORM wore on. Ryan sat in his bedroom, playing video games and watching the lightning crackle and spark in the distance. Their house sat on the top of a small hill. From his second-floor window he could see over the nearby rooftops and into the valley that lay beyond.

The rumbling storm clouds rose like a craggy mountain range on the horizon. Ryan thought of a powerful god, enraged at humanity, who was going to wipe out every man, woman and child. As he watched the storm front grind closer, he thought he heard muttered threats in the whooping wind. Warnings? A sign of danger to come?

That was crazy. Storms didn't warn people, and they didn't have voices. They weren't a sign of anything except a cloud full of electrical charges looking for something to zap.

He knew what he was doing, and he didn't like it. He was worrying too much about Abby. Again. He often wondered what it'd be like to have a normal sister. Someone who wasn't picked on all the time, pushed around in the hallways, called names. It was no wonder Abby took refuge in the school library every chance she got. Or so he heard from his friends' younger siblings, the kids he secretly paid off with Skittles and M&Ms to watch Abby at school.

When she had any free time at school, she could usually be found sitting among the stacks, looking at books with weird titles like, *The Encyclopedia of*

Mythological Beasts, Haunted Heartland of America, or *How to Create Your Own Magical Amulet.*

Sure, it was cool to watch Harry Potter movies, but most kids he knew didn't study the stuff. Or spend *all* their free time reading about people burned at the stake or demons abducting young children in the middle of the night. In fact, he didn't know *anyone* else into paranormal stuff as much as Abby.

One day, his father asked Ryan to privately keep an eye on Abby, though he never fully explained what "keep an eye on" meant. He just assumed it meant to protect her from bullies. And so that's what he did the day he got into a fight on the bus with Joey Hollister, an eighth grader who kept calling his sister "Spook."

That name stung Abby deeply, though she wouldn't talk about it. She wouldn't talk to anyone, not even Ryan, for a week after that.

Could he really blame anyone for thinking Abby was spooky? No, but that didn't give them a right to tease her. He wasn't sorry for the fight, or for the detention he got from the principal. He was just doing what any big brother who cared about his little sister would do.

Feeling claustrophobic, he turned off his Xbox and left his bedroom. Spending too much time in his own head made him crazy.

On his way to join his family downstairs, he took a detour without even realizing it. He found he did this often, his legs operating on autopilot, carrying him to his parents' room.

He knocked on the door and got a mumbled response.

He winced, feeling terrible. He woke his mother up. She was probably taking one of her now infamous long naps. It quickly went from a quick lie down a few months ago to a full-blown marathon sleeping session every afternoon.

Of course, he didn't blame her; who could? She needed the rest. Her body was fighting cancer.

When the oncologist revealed it to their family six

months ago, Ryan felt the bottom drop out of his world and a long black tunnel open up. The life of a teenager—friends, hanging out, studying for tests— suddenly felt like the least important thing in the world. But his mother had talked him out of this attitude very quickly. She promised him she could fight the cancer growing in her bones much more effectively if she knew her family was staying intact, both physically and emotionally. He promised through a sheen of tears that he'd keep going with his life and his studies, including sticking with basketball and the swim team.

For a while he managed it quite well, and then his mother took a turn for the worse. The chemotherapy wore her out, she lost her hair and her appetite, and some days she was too weak to lift her head up off the pillows. Then would come the good days. The "sunny ones," she would call it. On those days she was able to get up and even nibble a little food at the table with them, smile, listen to their stories about their days, and laugh. They almost seemed like a whole, intact family again on those days. Almost. But Ryan knew those days would never last, and the clouds would roll back in.

Ryan opened the door slowly and stuck his head inside the stuffy room. The blinds were drawn, and the heavily shadowed room had the damp smell of sweat and medicine. His mother turned her head to look at him. She smiled, lifting Ryan's spirits. He was afraid she'd be angry with him for waking her.

"Come in," she said, waving him forward. "I was just getting up…"

"You don't have to." He came around to her side of the bed and sat down. "I just wanted to …"

"What?" she asked when he hesitated. She stroked his cheek. Her hand felt cold and clammy, and Ryan squeezed it in his own.

"This trip we're taking tomorrow," he began. "We don't have to—I mean, I can stay here with you if you need me."

She smiled at him. "You've always been a thoughtful boy, and I love you for that. No, I want you to go. You deserve to go and have fun. I'll be all right, I promise. The sun is coming back tomorrow, I can feel it."

Ryan smiled back reflexively, but he was feeling anything but happy. He'd heard her say the sun was coming back now for the last two weeks, but still her condition seemed darker every day.

"Okay, Mom."

"Besides, who will watch out for your sister?" she added with a grin. "You're the only one she'll talk to most of the time. Or trust."

She was right, but lately he'd overheard Abby and his mother talking plenty of times behind the closed door. Once he lingered in the hall to hear what they were saying. He felt guilty eavesdropping on their private conversation, but Abby would never tell him what they talked about. He was curious what she might know about their mother's condition, what knowledge she might have about her future.

There I go again, thinking of Abby like she's a mind reader or fortune teller. But wasn't she? How else could he explain the things he'd seen her do?

"I'll keep her safe," Ryan promised.

"I know you will." She paused. "She looks up to you, you know."

He was taken aback.

"Don't look so surprised, Ryan. She knows you're her protector, but it won't be a job you'll have forever. Some day she's going to grow up to be …" Here she hesitated, choosing her words carefully. "To be someone who will light the world up."

Light the world up. Yes, he could see that. Someday.

He kissed his mother on the forehead and turned to leave. "Get some rest," he said.

"I will," she sighed, her eyelids fluttering shut.

Ryan watched her for a moment before easing out of the room. As he was about to close the door, he heard her speak again, and he froze.

"The magic is in the box," she murmured.

Ryan looked in on her again, but she was fast asleep. What did she mean? What box? Could she have been sleep-talking? Abby did that sometimes, mumbling incoherent things under her breath while she slept. Feeling uneasy, he closed her door and went downstairs.

Chapter 3

R YAN FOUND HIS family in the kitchen. Abby
was sitting at the table eating dinner, which
consisted of french fries, yogurt, and a slice of
deli ham—a typical Abby meal. She was devouring the
french fries first, because, alphabetically speaking, they
had to go first.

Abby wore a long purple T-shirt with pink stripes
and green shorts. Ryan cringed at her complete lack of
fashion sense. Her face was pink and freshly

scrubbed from the bath she'd just taken. She fingered a strand of wet blond hair. Ryan recognized the habit; it meant she was deep in thought about something.

"I just don't know this one." His father sat beside Abby, tapping a pen against his chin and mulling over a crossword puzzle. "'Grow strong.' Any idea, Abby? It starts with a C. Ten letters."

"Dad," he interrupted, "you're asking an eleven year old for help on a crossword puzzle? You must be pretty desperate. I mean, I know she's smart, but I don't think . . ."

"Convoloo!" Abby blurted. At least that's what it sounded like around a mouthful of french fries.

Dad frowned. "Can you please repeat that after you swallow your food?"

Abby finished chewing and took a swig of milk. When she was done, she said, "Convalesce. To recover one's health after an illness or medical treatment."

Dad stared incredulously at Abby, glanced down at the crossword puzzle, and broke out in a wide grin. "That's it! I'm almost finished. Let's see . . . 'a concealed idea.' Eight letters. Second letter is a b and the fourth is a t. Do you know it, Abby?"

"Why doesn't Abby play normal games like normal kids do?" Ryan said, digging through the refrigerator for a Coke.

"Abstruse!" Abby exclaimed, her finger jutting in the air. "Difficult to understand!"

"Figures you'd know that one," Ryan muttered.

"We were playing checkers earlier," Dad said as he filled in the word, "but Abby got bored with the game. She's really good at crossword puzzles. I think you would be too if you gave them a chance."

"They're boring," he stated bluntly. He sat down at the table with his drink and snatched a french fry from Abby's plate when she wasn't looking. "You have to sit for too long and think. I hate thinking. Makes my brain itch." He took a bite of the french fry and almost gagged. As usual, Abby put enough salt on her food to choke a horse.

Abby fixed her flat, unwavering gaze on him. "You don't hate thinking," she told him.

"Oh? How do you know?"

"You were playing video games a little while ago, weren't you? Probably *Zombie Kingdom*, your favorite. You amassed a lot of points, destroyed a lot of zombies, all without taking a hit. Until you met your nemesis, King Zombie, himself. He always outwits you."

Amassed? Nemesis? Outwits? What kind of fifth grader talked that way? Even his high-school friends didn't know most of Abby's words, and some of them were honor students!

Ryan shrugged. "If by 'outwit' you mean he beat me, then yeah, King Zombie is pretty tough. He has eight heads! No one knows how to kill him, and some of my friends play the game every day."

"Well," she said, picking up a french fry, inspecting

26

it, and setting it back down on her plate. "You were *thinking* when you played the game, only you didn't realize it. Your subconscious was looking for patterns in how the zombies attacked, and you made quick decisions about which weapon to use. In time, through trial and error, you'll master the matrix of the game, and then you'll defeat King Zombie. Of course, there are loftier pursuits."

He hadn't seen his little sister this talkative in a long time. "'Loftier pursuits?'" He looked her in the eye. "Name one."

"I'll name one soon." she said cryptically.

"When?"

"Soon."

"How soon?"

"Maybe next week. Maybe tomorrow."

"Another *forecast*, like the rain this afternoon?" He grinned.

Abby said nothing.

"I thought you knew everything."

"That's enough," Dad snapped. "Don't tease your sister."

"It's okay, Dad," she said, sprinkling more salt on her fries. "I'm used to it."

Ryan felt a stab of regret for what he'd said. Autism or no, there was still something mysterious about the way her brain worked. It was like she had a locked room in the attic of her mind, and within that locked room were secrets. She knew things that no one should rightly know. She called those moments of insights *forecasts*. Like an old gypsy gazing into a crystal ball, she claimed she could see things and predict the future. Like last week, when she predicted where exactly they'd find Jasper, their goldendoodle, when he'd slipped through a hole in the fence and ran away. *On a farm outside of town, running circles around an old abandoned well.* Who could have possibly known? The odds of guessing that and being correct were astronomical.

And then the forecast that afternoon, predicting

rain out of a clear blue sky.

Sometimes, she didn't seem to be aware of her own powers. It was as if the door in her mind had its own inexplicable voodoo. It opened on loose hinges at unexpected moments that seemed to catch even Abby off guard. In his opinion, it was the craziest thing about his sister—and the scariest, too.

After all, if *she* wasn't in complete control of that wondrously complicated mind of hers, then what was?

"Well," Dad said, folding the newspaper, "we should be getting off to bed soon. We leave first thing in the morning."

"What about Mom?" The question was out of Ryan's mouth before he could stop it.

Dad stared at him sympathetically. "She needs to stay here and rest. Your Aunt Kim is coming over to stay with her while we're gone this weekend." He paused. "I know it won't be the same without her, but she insists we go."

Their father was right. She did insist, many times

over this past week, that they take the trip without her. She'd be fine, she assured them. After all, it was only for the weekend. At first their dad protested and said there was no way they were leaving without her, that Uncle Silas would understand.

Their mother almost gave in.

Then came the late-night chats with Abby, ones that would end sometimes with their mother weeping softly, other times with her giggling happily. Ryan wished he knew what they were saying together, but no matter how many times he approached Abby about these secret tête-à-têtes, she wouldn't tell him anything. The most he got from her was that she was giving Mom advice. Advice about what? he'd ask. She'd only gaze past him and shrug. At this point he'd get angry with her for holding out, but truthfully, he wished he had the bond with their mother that Abby did.

"What time are we leaving?" Ryan asked.

"Bright and early. Six o'clock. It's about a five-hour drive to the Adirondacks, and last time we almost got lost, remember?"

"We did get lost," Ryan corrected.

"Well, it won't happen this time. I've got GPS."

Actually, they had GPS two years ago when they visited Uncle Silas at his tucked-away-in-the-middle-of-nowhere cabin deep in the mountainous woods, but even the satellites got confused trying to find his place.

"I can't wait to get there," Ryan said.

Dad took his cellphone out of his pocket. "I think he has something special planned for us when we get up there. He sounded pretty eager on the phone last week, practically insisting that we come and spend a few days with him. I better call him and let him know when to expect us."

Dad punched the number into his cell as Abby stared quizzically at him, her head cocked to one side like she was straining to hear something.

Ryan couldn't wait to go fishing in the lake near his

uncle's house because he always seemed to catch a boatload of bass, trout, and bluegill. It was like hitting the jackpot every time. He also enjoyed the long hikes in the woods and the campfires. And while he'd never admit it to his friends, being out of wi-fi range for a few days wasn't such a bad thing.

"That's strange," Dad said, holding the phone away from his ear. They listened as high-pitched squawking, followed by a series of staticky noises like rushing water, came through the phone's tiny speaker. Then the noise abruptly cut off and the cell went dead.

"What is it, Dad?" Ryan asked.

"I don't know." He shook his head and frowned. "The phone rang a couple of times, then it stopped like somebody answered it. Next, all I heard were a few weird clicks and scrapes like somebody scratching the phone with their fingernails, then a lot of noise."

Still frowning, he called again.

"Nothing," he said, staring at the phone as if waiting for an explanation. "The line is dead."

"I guess we'll find out tomorrow," Ryan said. He felt an icy chill caress his spine.

"Probably just a downed line," Dad responded reasonably. "The weathermen said this is a huge storm system, stretching all the way from here to Central New York. Yeah, that must be it."

Dad stepped over to the window and gazed out at the pitchforks of lightning splitting the sky. He shook his head. "It sure is nasty out there."

For the next few seconds, they all listened in silence to the drumming rain, then Abby whispered: "Enigma."

Ryan stared at her.

"What was that, sweetie?" Dad asked.

"Enigma," she repeated. "A mysterious or puzzling thing or event."

Nobody disagreed.

Chapter 4

ATER THAT NIGHT, after everyone had gone to bed, Ryan heard a faint knock on his bedroom door.

He sat up and rubbed his eyes. As he adjusted to the dark, he could make out the hulking shape of his dog on the floor next to his bed. Jasper stirred, scratched lazily at an itch on the back of his neck, rolled over, and went back to sleep.

Ryan listened for the knocking sound again. Nothing. Maybe he dreamt it. His nerves were a little edgy after the phone call that evening. Sighing, he rolled over onto his side and pulled the sheet up over his head.

And that's when he felt it.

A tapping on his shoulder.

Startled, he jerked the covers off and sat bolt upright in bed. "What—who's there?"

"*Quiet,*" a small voice insisted. "You'll wake Mom and Dad."

Standing next to his bed with a flashlight pointed up at her face was Abby. The light made her eyes look black and sunken, like the face of a hideous Jack-o'-lantern.

He fought back his anger at the unexpected intrusion. Didn't she realize an athlete needed his sleep? He was about to open his mouth to explain this to her when she put a finger to her lips. "Shhh!" Next, she brought her other hand out from behind her back, in which she held a small bowl of water. For a moment he thought she was holding Jasper's water dish.

Then he realized it was something different.

Abby sunk to the floor and sat cross-legged, resting the bowl in her lap. It was senseless to refuse the invitation to join her. He knew she would sit like that, a meditating tween monk, until he joined her. Abby was patient to a fault.

Sighing, he slid out of bed and joined her.

"You know it's two-thirty in the morning, don't you?"

Abby blinked. Clearly, the information was irrelevant to her.

"What's that for?" he asked, changing the subject. "Are we making soup?"

"It's a scrying bowl," she answered, ignoring his lame joke. She took three candles out of the pocket of her nightgown and set them on the floor.

"Are you sad?"

"No, not crying, *scrying*. You use it to see the future. Nostradamus used one all the time."

"Nostra-who?"

"Nostradamus. A prophet who lived in sixteenth-century France. He was well known for his quatrains that predicted the future."

His sister, the human encyclopedia.

"Okay," he said, shaking his head. "I'll bite. What does this have to do with us?"

"Something is wrong with Uncle Silas. I just *know* it, but I don't know exactly *what*. Maybe we can see it in the scrying bowl."

"How does it work?"

"We concentrate."

"That's it? Just concentrate?"

"And believe."

"In what?"

Abby looked at him patiently. "In the power of the mind to recognize magic when it sees it. And the heart to deliver its power. That's hard for you to understand, isn't it?"

He glanced down at the bowl. With his eyes now fully adjusted to the dark and with the help of a little moonlight leaking into the room, he could see the bowl gleamed like it was made of some kind of metal.

How on Earth was a bowl of water going to tell them the future? On the heels of that thought came another: *What is my sister doing with a scrying bowl, and where did she get it?*

No sooner had he thought this than a possible answer popped into his head: Uncle Silas. He remembered seeing things like the scrying bowl at his cabin before. Along with Tarot cards, wooden blocks with runes etched on them, and other, New Age-y stuff. And Abby always seemed fascinated by their uncle's mysterious apothecary.

While he thought about this, he didn't notice Abby's hands. Suddenly, a bright flame jumped to life. She touched the match to the tip of the first candle and held it there until the wick caught.

"You're not supposed to have matches!" Ryan admonished her as she positioned the candle next to the scrying bowl. He knew he sounded like their father, but he didn't care. "We could get in trouble!"

Abby regarded him with a bland look. "I know you won't tell." She was right, of course; he wouldn't tell. Unless she burned down the house, then all bets were off.

Ryan watched as Abby lit the two remaining candles. She placed them in a triangular pattern around the scrying bowl. When she was done, the room was bathed in an eerie orange glow. He could see the bowl even better. Definitely bronze or copper, no bigger than a cereal bowl, and adorned around the outside with strange shapes and symbols. The water inside looked murky, bottomless, like the mouth of a deep well. A trick of the light, no doubt. Had to be.

Abby peered intently at the water. Ryan waited, holding his breath, uncertain what to expect. He honestly expected nothing to happen, because how could it? This was a silly child's game. He figured she'd look up at him in a few seconds and declare the whole thing a failure. At which point, he'd do what any good big brother would do, which is get his odd little sister a glass of milk and send her to bed.

He was already thinking of something sympathetic to say to her when the surface of the water rippled slightly. Abby's hands weren't anywhere near the bowl.

Next, a tiny whirlpool in the center of the water began spinning in a counterclockwise direction, as though stirred by an invisible finger.

Jasper, sensing something amiss, growled from deep inside his chest.

"What's going on?" he whispered.

Abby ignored the question and closed her eyes. She held her hands palms down over the bowl and started murmuring these words:

"Show the future, share with me
The mysteries of time.
What will happen I will see,
And your secrets shall be mine."

Abby repeated the words several times, all the while slowly moving her hands together in a circular motion above the scrying bowl. He watched the water closely, fighting the urge to get up and run. When a minute passed and nothing more happened, Abby opened her eyes and gazed at the bowl, disappointed. Then she said, "Maybe it would help if you said the words with me."

Ryan rolled his eyes. "Maybe it would help if we got some sleep."

"You need to believe for this to work, Ryan."

"I think you're going to have to believe for both of us, Abs."

Abby sighed and shut her eyes again. She resumed chanting the words while Ryan sat back and watched, amused.

He never understood magic. What was the point? Magic was when a guy pulled your card out of a deck, or made a pretty girl disappear in a box and reappear in another. Now *that* was cool. But magic was nothing more than illusion, parlor tricks, smoke and mirrors, and mind games.

For the first time he felt real pity for his sister. Was she ever going to grow out of her obsession with fantasy?

He was about to tell her to leave his room once and for all when something in the water caught his attention. A sudden flicker of movement.

A small black minnowy shadow darted across the bottom.

Then it happened again, a flash of motion, followed by a quick burst of sparkling light.

There was something in the water— although *in* was not accurate. It was like looking through a watery window at a world slowly coming into focus on the other side.

Ryan gasped. "What is *that*?"

Abby stopped chanting and looked at the scrying bowl. Her eyes lit up in rare excitement. "I see it, too!"

She bent over the bowl until her face was almost

touching the water, but the shiny light and the darting shadow were both gone. The bowl of water was just a bowl of water again. Disappointed, she sat back and groaned. He didn't want to be the one to tell her, but he knew this was a colossal waste of time.

"There was something there," she started to say, "but I couldn't focus on it."

"I think it was a trick of the light. The candles were flickering and causing shadows. Then when you leaned forward you blocked the light and the illusion vanished."

She disagreed. "It was a vision. Something dark, like an animal or a bird. In many cultures, the sight of a crow or raven signifies death."

"Is that what you saw? A raven?" I couldn't keep the sarcasm out of my voice.

"You can make fun of me if you want," she replied. "I don't care."

"I wasn't making—"

He cut himself off when another dark shadow

43

flitted beneath the water's surface. An image slowly came into focus. Riveted, Abby and Ryan held their breaths as the dark silhouettes of trees emerged. A forest. Violent wind whipsawed the trees back and forth. A figure emerged from the forest, streaking toward them. An animal of some sort …

The water suddenly blackened. It roiled and bubbled on the surface, spilling over the rim of the bowl. The candles guttered as an icy breeze shot across the room. Abby lunged backwards in terror, gripped the sides of her face, and screamed at the top of her lungs.

A blackbird erupted from the scrying bowl and shot upwards toward the ceiling. Its ear-splitting cry echoed all around them. Jasper barked like crazy, jumping and snapping at the bird. The bird dove at their heads twice before swooping toward the window, which it struck with so much bone-crunching force that it shattered the glass.

Footsteps rushed down the hall toward Ryan's

room.

"What is going on in here?" Dad shouted as he threw open the door.

"Abby!" Their mother walked unsteadily into the room behind him, her face flushed with panic. Ryan watched as his terrified sister buried her face in their mother's shoulder and cried inconsolably.

Dad scowled at Ryan, whose face burned with anger and humiliation. His father didn't have to say it; the accusation was written plainly all over his face. *Whatever is going on here, son, you could have done more to stop it. You know your sister.*

Ryan was exhausted, all he wanted to do was get back into bed and forget the whole thing happened, but there was a dead bird with a broken neck lying on the floor that needed to be tended to first.

"Are you all right, Abby?" Dad sniffed the air. "Anything you want to tell us?"

Abby wiped her eyes. "I just had a fright, that's all."

Jasper let loose one more jittery bark and then

scampered out of the room.

Mom brushed the long hair out of her daughter's face. "What are you doing in Ryan's room so late, and how did the window break?"

"It was this." Their father pointed out the broken body of the raven lying in front of the window.

"How did a *bird* get in here?" their mother wanted to know, staring strangely at Abby.

Abby's gaze dropped to the scrying bowl on the floor. The water inside it had returned to normal, clear and undisturbed. Mom picked it up and stared at it. "What is this?"

"Uncle Silas gave it to me a long time ago," replied Abby.

"That doesn't answer my question."

Abby stared serenely at Mom, her eyes completely dry, and her voice returned to its oddly monotone cadence. "It's a scrying bowl, Mom. Like we talked about before."

Amazed, Ryan watched his mother's expression

soften as understanding dawned on her face. Without a word, she returned the scrying bowl to Abby.

"Let's go back to bed," she said, reaching for her husband's arm for support. "I'm exhausted."

"Of course." Their father led her to the door and out into the hall, but not before turning around to glare at Ryan one more time.

"I don't know what exactly you two were doing in here or why you were burning candles in the middle of the night, but right now you're both going to clean up this mess. We'll discuss what happened in the morning."

Chapter 5

BACK IN HER bedroom, Abby waited until the voices of her parents faded and the house grew quiet again before she got out of bed and went to her window.

She hoped Ryan wouldn't take all the blame for what happened tonight. It wasn't his fault. Besides, she didn't need him to use the scrying bowl—his energy was usually very negative anyway. She just didn't want to be alone. She had a sense something was going to happen that she might not be able to control.

But the horror that she experienced … it was like nothing she'd ever felt before. It came over her with unexpected intensity. She knew she was different from other kids and didn't feel what they felt or care about the things they cared about. She truly was *quirky*, as her brother liked to say. Yet there was nothing she could do about it.

She brooded at the window for another few minutes, listening to the grumbling belly of the storm as it crawled overhead.

The vision she saw in the scrying bowl haunted her thoughts. Every time she closed her eyes, she saw it flitting across the water again, its black wings soaring past a muddy sky.

It meant to attack them.

Harm them.

Possibly even kill them.

What had sent it? Abby sensed there was a

powerful, and *deadly*, force behind the attack. Some unknown power connected in some way to her uncle.

Abby didn't know what the connection was, but she knew he was in trouble. And somehow she and Ryan were involved in this, too. When Abby reached out with her mind to her uncle, a trick she used to make her infamous *forecasts*, she met a wall of resistance, a force that pushed back.

This wall of active energy, created by something dark and powerful that surrounded her uncle and jealously guarded him, was unbreakable, no matter how hard she pushed.

She tried again now, squeezing her eyes shut and calling the image of her uncle to mind. She focused so hard that a tiny ache started in the middle of her forehead, but nothing happened. No mental pictures emerged. She did the trick just like Uncle Silas had taught her, the way he'd learned it from *his* father, and so on. *Mind waves,* he'd called it. Sort of a built-in cell phone of the brain.

Abby sighed and returned to her bed, drawing the sheets up to her chin. She didn't think she could sleep, however. She felt wide awake and alert, her body a hive of buzzing energy.

But at some point she began to settle down. Her tension melted away, and exhaustion crept over her. She was sinking deeply into the quicksand of sleep when ...

Abby jumped and sat bolt upright in bed, looking around her room. Who or what was there? She realized she wasn't lying in her bed anymore. And her house had disappeared, too. She was in her uncle's cabin, sprawled on a couch in his ransacked living room, staring at an unbelievable mess.

Vials and jars of preserved herbs and medicines were shattered on the floor. Chairs were overturned. Tables knocked over. Books flung all about the place with reckless abandon. Abby surveyed the wreckage with dismay. Who would have done such a thing? But the more urgent question was why was she being shown all this? Who had brought her here?

As Abby crossed the room, something caught her attention outside. She peered through the rain-streaked window and saw a shadowy silhouette of a hunched figure and two large dogs or wolves dragging something into the woods.

Lightning flashed suddenly, and Abby had a clearer view of the person on the ground. Her uncle's eyes were closed, and he had streaks of blood running down his face and into his long white beard. Abby called out to him, though the howl of the storm drowned out her words.

To her surprise the hunched figure did stop walking and turned back to stare at the cabin. At *her*. Abby dropped out of sight from the window, but it was too late; she had already been seen. She peeked through a corner of the glass and saw the figure with flowing black hair and blazing eyes staring directly at her. A jolt of panic shot through Abby's body. What if the wolves came back for *her*? But a few seconds later, the woman and her beasts continued dragging her uncle into the woods and disappeared.

Abby screamed, tearing the nightmare to shreds, but she found no comfort at all in being wide awake and safe in her own bed. The dream was all too real.

A warning meant just for her.

Chapter 6

MORNING BROKE with glorious sunshine and sparkling blue sky. The storm had retreated far to the north, leaving deep puddles and a trail of leafy carnage through their backyard. It was like any another summer storm, except something he couldn't name suggested to Ryan this storm would be back.

While their dad loaded their Subaru Outback, Ryan sat in the kitchen eating breakfast slowly, spooning Fruit Loops into his mouth without even tasting them. Last night's adventure weighed heavily on his mind. He was worried about his sister.

Abby had come to him first thing in the morning with an incredible tale, even for her. She believed her nightmare had really happened, and that she had triggered a psychic connection between herself and whatever happened to Uncle Silas. She actually believed she had been teleported to his cabin last night. That was her word for it—*teleported*. He couldn't help cracking up. It reminded him too much of Dungeons and Dragons, a game he used to play almost every day with his geeky friends when he was a kid.

Ryan assured his sister it was just a dream, and that dreams could seem very real. There was no reason to believe anything had happened to Uncle Silas, just because his phone wasn't working last night. But she insisted he was wrong.

"You know you have an overactive imagination, don't you?" he said. But as soon as the words left his mouth, he regretted them.

"How can you say that?" Abby cried. "Or did you

already forget that a raven flew out of the scrying bowl and shattered your window?"

Ryan shushed her before her screeching could wake up their mom. He was feeling bad enough already about going on this vacation without her.

"I didn't forget anything," he replied in a low voice. "I was the one who had to take the bird and its broken neck outside and throw it in the field, and then clean up broken glass. I had to sleep downstairs on the couch because my room was too cold and the rain was blowing in!"

Abby didn't say anything more. Ryan let it drop, too. Getting her upset all over again wouldn't accomplish anything. He was still tense about last night. He turned it over again and again in his mind but couldn't come up with any answer for the raven. How did a bird get into his room?

It happened to people sometimes, didn't it? The power of suggestion, that sort of thing? After all the times he'd listened to his crazy sister talking about ghosts and witches and supernatural stuff, it was bound to pollute his imagination. That had to be it, he decided. At least, it was an explanation he could live with.

That raven's neck was pretty busted up, a voice in his head reminded him. *The bones felt like ball bearings rolling around in a greasy sack, remember?*

True, he answered the voice. *But it was dark, and the bird was probably already in my room.*

Yeah, right.

A moment later he heard his father calling for him. Ryan bolted the rest of his breakfast and ran out the back door, where he found his dad standing at the back of the car.

"Need help, Dad?" he asked.

"I got it, thanks." His father put the last suitcase in the trunk. He gave everything a final once-over and then shut the door. Then he looked up at Ryan.

"Long night last night."

"Yeah." Ryan stared down at his shoes. "You

could say that."

"Your mother was pretty worried."

"Yeah. Well, it's okay now."

"Is it?" His dad nudged his arm. "What exactly happened last night?"

"Mom asked you to interrogate me?"

"It's not like that. We're just concerned—*I'm* concerned. I've never seen Abby so upset like that before. What frightened her so much? I mean, besides the bird."

Why does she do half the things she does? he wanted to ask, but he bit his tongue. He'd asked the question out loud before, numerous times in fact, but the answer he always got was a lesson on the quirkiness of spectrum disorders and the different ways the human brain functions. The bottom line was, no one knew exactly what went on in that mysterious Fun House brain of Abby's, and no one ever would.

"Honestly, I don't know," Ryan admitted. "She has an overactive imagination."

"That's putting it kindly." His father smiled.

"I'm not sure what was happening."

"Then what did you *see*?"

Ryan realized they were both almost whispering, which didn't surprise him. Abby had been known to hear conversations outside of the normal earshot of people.

He turned away and shrugged. How could he answer his dad's question? The question was a trap anyway. Whatever he said, it was bound to sound certifiably crazy coming out of his mouth.

He was the practical sibling, wasn't he? The athlete. Not exactly Oxford material, but smart in a practical, everyday sort of way. If all went according to plan, he would be going to college in a year to study engineering. Maybe go to work for NASA, something like that. He'd always been good working with his hands, assembling and disassembling things, noticing how all the parts fit together.

Except for Abby. He couldn't for the life of him

figure out what made her tick.

If he told his dad the truth, that Abby was trying to see into the future like Nostradamus but instead saw something they both couldn't explain, he'd accuse Ryan of lying to protect his sister. Or lying to get her into trouble.

His dad might have spent his waking hours researching and writing books about legends, myths and the occult, but that didn't mean he necessarily believed in all of it.

Seeing that his son wasn't ready to talk yet, he tried a different tact. "You know I expect you to keep an eye on your sister this weekend, right?"

Ryan nodded. "I always do."

"She clings to you whenever she's in public, and she looks up to you."

"Trust me, I know."

"So, if she gets into any trouble, has any more frights like last night ..."

"I'll tell you."

He smiled. "Abby is a special person, Ryan. And I know she has unusual habits that annoy you sometimes. Her interest in magic, the occult…I think we both know where she gets it from."

Ryan thought of his mother lying upstairs in bed. And her father's brother, their great Uncle Silas.

"It's all just make-believe," Ryan said with a shrug. He was unsure which of them he was trying to convince more.

Dad tousled his hair. "Hey, what do you say you go in and say good-bye to your mother. And hurry your sister up! I'd like to hit the road in a few minutes."

Relieved to have something to do, Ryan bounded into the house and up the stairs to Abby's room. On the way, he heard whispery voices coming from behind his parents' bedroom door. He crept to the door, put his ear to the wood, and listened.

"I'll find it and bring it back," he heard Abby say.

"In the box," his mother responded weakly. "It'll

be in the box."

"Where?"

Ryan heard her give a deep, rattling cough before answering. "I don't know where he put it."

"I'm scared for Uncle Silas, Mom."

"He can handle himself," his mother said confidently. "His powers are greater than you know."

Ryan was about to open the door and stopped when he heard his name mentioned.

"And one last thing, Abby. Stick close to Ryan. He loves you and will keep you safe."

"Ryan doesn't understand," Abby said.

His mother mumbled something he didn't catch. He leaned in closer to the door.

"I had a vision."

He heard his mother's sharp intake of air.

"What are you talking about?"

"What I saw in the scrying bowl last night," Abby replied. "It was a vision. I think something bad has happened to Uncle Silas."

"Then maybe you shouldn't go—"

"I need to go."

"What do you mean?"

"I think I'm the only one who can save him … and you."

"Abby …"

His mother broke down into another coughing fit. Ryan waited, but when it seemed like they were done talking, he cleared his throat and knocked on the door.

"Abby? You in there?"

He opened the door slowly and found Abby standing by their mother's bed. She wore a worried look. He hesitated before entering any further, afraid he was intruding, but his mother waved him over with a smile.

"We were just saying good-bye," she said, then added, "I'm sure your father is getting antsy."

"Yeah," Ryan answered. "I just wanted to tell you we were leaving."

"I know." Their mother glanced at Abby, who

immediately turned and left the bedroom.

"I'll be in the car," she said, as her footsteps echoed down the hall.

"I love you," their mother called after her, but in customary Abby fashion, the sentiment was ignored.

Love was an emotion Abby understood intellectually, and probably even appreciated, but was incapable of expressing herself.

Ryan gave his mom's hand a squeeze. He suddenly felt awkward, and the chilling thought that this was a final farewell of sorts kept nagging at him.

"Are you all right?" she asked him.

Ryan didn't know what to say at first. It was an odd question for her to be asking. She was the one with the cancer, after all, not him.

"Fine."

"Take care of your sister."

"I will," he replied. "I always do."

"I know."

A question came to him, but as he was about to

ask it, a strange look settled on his mother's face. Her features smoothed to the point where her face looked blank, but an earnestness glowed bright in her eyes. He tried to pull his hand away from hers, but her suddenly painful vice-like grip tightened around his fingers. He found himself entranced by her penetrating gaze, and he couldn't move, couldn't take a breath. Then a whisper floated in the air behind him—or maybe it was coming from inside his own head. It moved through his mind like a gentle current.

"Believe."

Ryan heard his mother's voice, but her lips hadn't moved at all. A tingle of fear chilled the nape of his neck.

"Mom?"

"The witch will come at night."

"What are you talking about?"

But she didn't answer. Instead, her eyes closed, and her hand went limp. She fell into a quick and sudden sleep, leaving Ryan with more questions but no time to ask them. Fortunately, he had Abby.

He hoped she would be able to explain what just happened.

Chapter 7

ABBY SAT IN the back seat as the car hummed along, a Sudoku book open on her lap. She was already half-done with the puzzle before they even reached the highway. Ryan watched with envy as she quickly scribbled numbers into the tiny boxes, never once having to erase. Not for the first time he wondered how those random numbers could pop into her head so easily, but then gave up wondering because it only made him want to beat his comparatively slow brain with a stick.

Ryan settled back in the front seat, preparing to slip his earbuds in and listen to some music, when his dad's voice stopped him. Dad was being a chatterbox today. Ryan knew he loved to talk about his work, but this time there seemed to be something else going on. His hands were restless on the wheel, and his left foot wouldn't stop tapping nervously on the floor. He must have been anxious about Uncle Silas, or worried about leaving Mom, or both.

Ryan couldn't blame him, especially after what happened last night.

"Did I ever tell you two the story about Theodore Roosevelt and the night he almost died up in these mountains?" Dad asked.

Several times, Ryan thought. But what he said was, "You might have mentioned it before."

"This happened back in 1915," he continued, ignoring the sarcasm. "Theodore Roosevelt, our vice president at the time, was hiking in the High Peaks region when word reached him that President

McKinley had been shot in Buffalo. Calling at once for his buckboard, Roosevelt rode down the High Peaks in the middle of the night, pushing those horses faster than they'd ever gone before. He needed to get to the train station in North Creek so he could get back to Buffalo as soon as possible. If McKinley died from his wounds, Theodore Roosevelt would become the next President.

"Well, mountain roads back then were narrow and steep; they're not much better today. They weren't meant to be traveled on in the dead of night by a team of wild horses. If you missed a turn, or the road gave out beneath your wheels, you could fall over the edge to a terrifying death below. More than once, the buckboard's wheels slipped. Roosevelt wrote in his personal journal that the trip was the most terrifying in his life. He believed he wouldn't live to see the bottom of the mountain. Although it was a white-knuckle ride, Roosevelt managed to get down the mountain in one piece."

"Did President McKinley die?" Abby asked, though she knew the answer already.

Dad nodded. "He died two days later from the gunshot wound. Theodore Roosevelt became the thirty-first President of the United States."

"Sad story, Dad," Ryan said.

"It proves one thing," he replied. "The mountains are dangerous, even for experienced outdoorsmen. And it's the things you don't expect to happen that will get you."

This story is for Abby, Ryan thought. She was the one who was good at stirring up mischief, like last night. Ryan knew it, and so did their father.

Ryan glanced back at Abby, who stared impassively out the window. *In one ear and out the other.*

Abby and Trouble had made their acquaintance last night, and he was sure their relationship was just getting started.

With that thought ping-ponging around in his head, Ryan eased the seat back and stretched out his lanky frame. He slipped in his earbuds and closed his eyes.

He waited to see if his dad was going to bring up last night or start another history lesson. Ryan hoped he'd just file last night's incident into the ever-growing folder of Strange Episodes Involving Abby and leave it at that.

After all, Abby was an *enigma*.

Fortunately, his father seemed lost in thought now and no longer in the mood to talk. Ryan turned on iTunes and cranked up the music. Between the deeply resonant bass lines and the steady vibration of the car's wheels on the blacktop, Ryan quickly felt the tension melt off his body. Last night drained all his energy, and something told him he'd need his strength for the next few days.

Go to sleep, he told himself.

And a moment later …

He is on a motorboat, slicing through the waves, the briny sea air filling his nostrils. Nothing around him but unbroken miles of ocean. No sign of land or people. He has the whole watery world to himself.

He stops the boat, drops the anchor, and then dives into the warm water. He swims deep, looping and twisting through the clear blue water, past schools of colorful fish and banks of bright coral. He looks up and sees a calm surface, a golden puddle of sunlight, and the dark cylindrical bottom of the boat. He kicks his legs to return to the surface when something heavy and strong wraps itself tightly around his leg. It stops him dead in the water, just a few feet from the boat. He thrashes wildly to break free, but his ankle is held in an iron grip. His hands reach desperately for the boat. Spiky tingles from oxygen-deprived muscles race up and down his arms and legs. Darkness closes around his vision.

He gives up trying to reach the boat, instead turning his attention to whatever has ensnared his leg. A pair of eyes stare up at him through the murk, stark white and deep-set, in a face of peeling green-black skin. Human eyes. The eyes of a hideous woman whose rotting corpse couldn't possibly be alive. She smiles, exposing two rows of jagged yellow teeth.

Curse of the Witch

Ryan screams in horror and starts kicking wildly to escape the thing's grasp. A clawed hand, gray and curved with bony knuckles, tugs on him again, pulling him deeper into the abyss. She—it—has incredible strength. He sinks with her, losing the will to fight. His head feels full and ready to explode. Little sparks of color bloom and dance before his eyes. He is drowning. He knows it but can't stop it. All he has the strength to do is watch as death welcomes him into its folds like a lazy blue whale swallowing a tuna.

He lets himself go.

His body is weightless.

And in the black of the water he finds peace…

Chapter 8

"RYAN, WAKE UP!"

He opened his eyes with a start. For one terrifying moment he thought he was dead, and the voice an angel's calling to him from the end of a long, bright tunnel. His heart was racing wildly, all the way up into his throat, which made him struggle for air. He looked around, surprised to find himself back in the car and wearing dry clothes.

Where had he gone? How did he get back here so quickly?

Then he realized the voice calling his name was his dad's, full of urgency and panic, and it jolted him to his senses. At the same time, he felt something sharp poking him in the ribs.

"Hey, that hurts!" Ryan pushed his sister's hand away. "What are you doing that for?"

"I'm waking you, obviously," she said, nonplussed. "You were dreaming."

Dad frowned. "More like having a nightmare. You were twisting and jumping like someone was attacking you!"

Ryan rubbed his eyes to get the image of the *thing* out of his head. "There *was* someone," he muttered in confusion. To his dismay, his ankle throbbed where her claws had grabbed him. "How long was I asleep?"

"Ten minutes," Abby informed him.

"What?" It felt more like hours.

"You were sleeping for ten minutes," she repeated. Then she leaned forward and whispered in his ear: "Was she wearing black?"

75

"Who?" he whispered back.

Abby narrowed her eyes. "You know who."

He stared at his sister as his insides coiled in horror. "How do you *know*?"

"You talk in your sleep," she replied with a shrug.

"What was it?" he asked her.

"You mean, *who* was it?"

"Hey, speak up," their dad interrupted. "What are you two whispering about?"

Abby didn't answer. She turned her attention back to the window and the rolling view of highway nothingness. A serene expression settled on her face. She was obviously not ready to tell anyone what she knew yet, but she would soon. Ryan would make sure of it. He needed to know what horror haunted their family—because now it was haunting *him*.

Ryan folded his arms and gazed out the window. Images of the ocean, of the lunatic thing with the empty eyes, were impressed on the backs of his eyelids. Whenever he blinked, the horror replayed itself frame-by-frame. The thing in the nightmare had tried to *kill* him. It wouldn't be the last time.

Interlude 1
What he finds in the dark

The old man prefers the idea of death to the place he finds himself in now.

He is in a cellar, lying on the damp earthen floor, with a sharp stone sticking into his back. He shifts his weight and fixes his attention on three slivers of light leaking through the floorboards above him.

It is morning—or maybe afternoon? What day is it? He has no watch on to tell him the time or date, but even if he did, the gloom is so thick he wouldn't have been able to read it.

Curse of the Witch

He keeps his eyes on the light. The light, he thinks, will give him hope and strength.

He is lucky to still be alive. Lucky the wolves that dragged him out of his cabin hadn't mauled him to pieces. Lucky he is still able to mutter a prayer of gratitude, thanking the merciful spirits of his ancestors for keeping him alive. He tries to sit up, but his body aches along his right side from being unceremoniously dumped into this hole, so he stays put and opens his senses to the darkness, which is empty though very much active.

The cellar stinks of mold and a sulfuric bitterness that irritates his nose and throat. He recognizes the smell at once: the lingering residue of black magic. Water drips on the ground somewhere nearby. He hears the ripple of wings and the sharp cries of ravens or crows, coming from another part of the house. And he hears the sharp claws of an animal—the wolves?—ticking along the floorboards above him.

Then the door at the top of the stairs creaks open, flooding the cellar with candlelight. The old man can do nothing but watch, his heart pounding fiercely, as the slight figure of a woman *with long, disheveled hair appears at the top of the steps and slowly thumps down the stairs to meet him.*

The reek of black magic surrounds her, its pungent odor so strong it makes the old man gag. She turns her face to him, and he gasps. If she were once a woman of any beauty at all, it had long ago wasted away, along with most of her flesh. What remains is a horror of mottled, diseased skin, and sunken eyes that glare from the recesses of her skull. Her feet shuffle on the steps, and her gait is slow and deliberate, as though she is trying to protect her aching bones from any undue stress that might shatter them.

He waits for her to tell him why he is here and what she wants. The thing on the stairs stops moving (he can't truthfully call it a woman anymore) and he hears it take a wet, rattling breath, and feels its inquisitive eyes crawling over his body. The old man has always been sensitive to auras, the invisible energy that surrounds living things. This creature's aura is black, blacker than the cellar itself, black enough to reveal evil intentions.

"SSSSiiiillllassss," the creature hisses.

The old man's body stiffens. It knows his name— Silas Martin—and probably knows a whole lot more about him as well. The voice is thin and reedy, like wind hissing through the tall grass.

Silas clears his throat. "I-I know who you are," *he stammers.* "I know what you did in Salem."

"You know nothing."

"I know I must stop you."

"You have no power over me now, Silas. You are the prisoner here."

The thing on the stairs stands mute for an uncomfortably long time, watching him, waiting. Waiting for what? He doesn't know, but it wants something, which might explain why it keeps him alive.

"What do you want from me?" *the old man finally croaks, his heart striking his ribs like a sledgehammer.*

The creature shifts and takes one more step down the darkened stairs.

"In two nights I'm going home, Silas," *she says.* "Home to Salem. I have ... unfinished business there."

The old man shudders. How has she grown so powerful so quickly? If she escapes, then a witch with incredible dark powers will be unleashed on mankind. He has to put a stop to it. If there were only a way...

The creature cackles. "Do not trouble yourself, Silas. There is nothing that can be done. The blood moon shall rise in two nights' time, and I will have my vengeance."

Abby could stop her, *he thinks.*

"The child? I think not."

The creature oozes along the cellar and stands over him in the dark.

"When I catch the girl, I will kill her, and then add her powers to mine."

The old man can smell the stink of the grave on her breath.

"And a true witch will walk the earth once again."

Part
Two

"A witch ought never to be frightened in the darkest forest, Granny Weatherwax had once told her, because she should be sure in her soul that the most terrifying thing in the forest was her."

Terry Pratchett, *Wintersmith*

Chapter 9

"LOOK AT THAT!" Dad pointed out the window. "Breathtaking, isn't it?"

Hours of driving were beginning to pay off. From a distance, the forest-clad mountains of the Adirondacks looked as delicate as a child's crepe-paper art project. Clouds scudded by, their immense shadows gliding along the peaks and valleys. It was a welcome sight. For the past three hours, they had seen nothing but fields of weeds, grass, and corn roll by. The occasional roadside fender-bender broke up the monotony, but overall the trip was tedious, and Ryan was beginning to feel trapped.

His heavy eyelids were trying to pull him down into another nap, but every time they did, he fought the urge by taking another slug of Mountain Dew Kickstart. The one-liter bottle he'd bought an hour ago at a Quicklee's gas-n-go was warm, but he didn't care. He wasn't drinking it for the flavor.

I know I can't stay awake forever, but I'll be damned if that thing gets her hands on me again!

He knew he was being silly about the nightmare. It was only a dream. A few neurons firing off random images. Still, it had felt so *real*, the creature's touch so *painful*.

And there was no mistaking the ring of dark bruises forming around his ankle. He rubbed them now, wondering if he should tell somebody.

Tell who? Dad? He wouldn't understand; and worse, he might decide to call the whole trip off and take his headcase kids back home. And that's exactly the kind of stress his mother

85

didn't need right now.

So, he kept the bruises and his fear of sleeping to himself. For now. Maybe he'd reevaluate later, after he had a chance to talk to Abby. Because Abby knew about such things.

Vivid nightmares, hallucinations, monsters, magic, and witches were in her repertoire, right up there with salty food and the Dewey Decimal System.

Sighing, Ryan eased back and relaxed a little as the environment transformed itself from vast highway emptiness to blossoming Adirondack beauty. Off in the distance tall stands of spruce and birch trees overshadowed low, marshy wetlands. Meadows filled with wildflowers crowded the road on either side of them. Abby's encyclopedic memory was able to recall a few of their names: trillium, lady's slipper, and Jack in the pulpit, along with clumps of bracken fern and sweet gale.

Ryan closed his eyes and tried to relax. With the sun on his face, he felt the grip of the bizarre dream begin to loosen.

He glanced back at Abby. She watched him with intense scrutiny. She hadn't stopped staring at him for the past hour. He knew she was being protective of him—a thought he found both amusing and irksome. *He* was supposed to be watching out for *her*, not the other way around. Whoever heard of a kid sister protecting her big brother?

Yet he couldn't deny there was a kind of comfort to it. Maybe it was superstitious thinking, but with Abby around he felt safe. Kind of like having a lucky rabbit's foot on his key chain. Not that he owned a rabbit's foot; he didn't believe in good luck charms, omens, or anything else superstitious.

In fact, he believed in making his own luck. As his father often said, quoting Benjamin Franklin: *Failure to prepare was preparing to fail.*

But after experiencing the raven in his bedroom— and the nightmare he'd had earlier—how could he deny the presence of *something* paranormal going on here? The rational part of him hated to admit it, but this vacation was already turning into something *otherworldly*. A thought that pleased him about as much as a summer book report.

Abby finally looked away when something caught her eye out the window. Dad was turning off the main drag and taking them up a narrow side street. Soon it would lead to Main Street, and after that, Uncle Silas's place.

He could recite the rest of the way from memory. Up ahead on the left would be a Methodist church with a tall white steeple and red doors. The message board in front of the church would contain a witty statement in tall black letters meant to inspire the faithful. Today it said:

GOD IS LIKE SCOTCH TAPE—
YOU CAN'T SEE HIM,
BUT HE STICKS AROUND!

As if on cue, a small woman hunched over a bed of zinnias in front of the sign looked up as we drove by and waved to us. Dad waved back.

"You know," he said, rolling down his window and taking a deep breath of the country air. "Life up here is simpler. People are happy to see you. Everything isn't rush, rush, rush. Makes me pine for the good ol' days before we all became glued to our computers and cell phones."

"How much longer till we get there?" Abby asked.

Dad smiled fondly at her and said, "Another few minutes, sweetheart. I'm going to stop at the general store first and get a few things."

"Aren't you worried about Uncle Silas?" Ryan asked.

"I'm sure he's fine."

"He hasn't called you."

"You forget, Ryan, how spotty the cell phone service is out here in the sticks. Besides, a lot of phone lines are going to be down after last night's storm.

Didn't you see the downed power lines a mile or so back up the road?"

He hadn't. His thoughts had been preoccupied.

The car chugged along. In another mile they came to a pinewood post with a wooden sign hanging off of it on rusty hinges. On the sign was the name of the little pioneering town that Uncle Silas called home. It read:

WELCOME TO BLACK ROCK FALLS!
HOME OF THE TALLEST TREES AND THE
FRIENDLIEST FOLK IN THE ADIRONDACKS!

Huge evergreen trees lined the road like sentinels, their low branches brushing the top of their car as it coasted by.

"Black Rock Falls used to be just a small farming community when it was established in 1718," said their father, returning to full scholarly mode again. "Times were tough for the first settlers. But soon more people started moving in, and the first sawmills and grist mills were built. Everyone had jobs. Before long, Black Rock Falls had schools, churches and stores. Fewer than two thousand people live here today, and I bet all of them know your uncle."

Ryan knew that last sentence was Dad's attempt at tongue-in-cheek humor. Uncle Silas made a living out of his cabin as a healer. Less a doctor and more a modern-day shaman, he created his potions and salves with homegrown herbs and plants and sold them to the locals. The inside of his little cabin looked like an apothecary in an old Western movie.

Apothecary was a word Abby had taught him. It meant a place where medicines were prepared and sold.

Sometimes people simply showed up on his doorstep and stayed for a cup of coffee, seeking only pleasant conversation. But most of the time, Uncle Silas told him, folks showed up late at night, and the ones who came after the moon rose were not there for companionship; they were desperate folks in need of a remedy, tincture, or concoction of some sort that Uncle Silas brewed up in his cabin. He'd cured broken hearts and broken limbs. Sometimes, when a midwife was out of town on the night in question, he'd even helped deliver babies. He'd seen more than a few residents of Black Rock Falls wail themselves into existence, he said with a chuckle. And, on occasion, wail themselves out.

Dad slowed as he turned onto Main Street. It hadn't changed at all from the last time they'd visited. It probably looked the same as it did when Uncle Silas was a kid. The street was short—short enough that you could walk the entire length of it on a hot day before your ice cream cone could begin to melt. A few cars were parked in front of the diner. Locals shuffled in and out of the barber shop, bank, and gas station. The steeple of an old Presbyterian church needled the sky. Across from it, on the other end of Main Street, sat a short, squat building set back from the road like it was trying to hide something. Its red paint was faded and peeling, and its roof was missing more than a few shingles. Yet the sign over the door read cheerfully: General Store. Goods of all Kinds. Come On In!

Their dad pulled up in front of the store and cut the engine. "You guys remember this place, don't you?" he asked.

Ryan and Abby both did. Shelf after shelf of toys, food, candy, T-shirts, locally made souvenirs, and the odd assortment of junk that sometimes—if you looked hard enough—yielded a treasure or two.

On their way inside the store, they stopped to read the community bulletin board attached to the wall next to the door. Their dad liked to read the pin-ups, which he said can give you a sense of the "local flavor" of a place. Ryan thought that was weird. He didn't know how you could learn anything about a town based on a collage of local advertisements and business cards. There were signs for free tutoring, housecleaning notices, and one for a local fishing derby happening next Saturday. The usual. But one thing did catch his eye, and Abby must have seen it at the exact same moment, because she started tugging on his sleeve.

"Look." She pointed to a colored picture of a cocker spaniel with the word LOST printed above it in huge letters. The owner who'd written the notice was desperate to find her "loving pet" as quickly as possible.

"There's more," Abby said, and she was right. A lot more. A goldendoodle named Ruby that went missing three nights ago, last seen up by Lake Road wearing a red collar and chasing after a squirrel. Another pet, a black cat named Buju, apparently wandered away one night and was never seen again. There were seven pets in all whose anxious owners wanted them back. And they all mysteriously disappeared sometime in the last two weeks.

"There's your local flavor, Dad," Ryan quipped, elbowing him. "Mass extinction of pets, happening right here in good ol' Black Rock Falls."

"You know that's not funny, right?"

Ryan chuckled to himself as he followed his dad and Abby inside.

Not surprisingly, the gift shop and supply store hadn't changed a bit since the last time they were here. It smelled like old cotton T-shirts, moth balls, and a faint industrial odor that could have been coming from the ancient ventilation system. The store was surprisingly well-stocked, however. The usual stuff—shirts, wind breakers, hats, paintings, framed photographs, and post cards—crowded the front of the store. As they moved toward the back, the items changed to fishing gear and basic outdoor equipment. On one wall was a display of hunting rifles; on the opposite wall were shelves stuffed with oddities and jars of weird things possibly dredged up from the bottom of nearby Black Rock Lake.

Their dad grabbed a few basic supplies for their stay and bought Ryan and himself new fishing rods and reels. (Abby, of course, looked down her nose at fishing.) She wandered over and scanned the one and only book rack in the place, picking one out and perusing the back cover. She brought it over and showed their dad.

"'Local Adirondack Lore and Legend,'" he read. "Sounds interesting. Would you read it?"

Abby stared at him. Asking her if she'd read a book was like asking a fish if it would swim in water.

Dad winked at her and added the book to the rest of his armload and took it up to the checkout counter.

"From out of town?" the old man behind the counter asked. He looked over their dad's selections before ringing them out like he'd never seen any of them before.

"Yes," Dad answered. "Coming up to stay a few days and visit my wife's uncle."

"What's his name?"

"Silas Martin."

The old man's face froze.

"Haven't seen him in two years," Dad added.

The old man's mouth twitched.

"You know Silas?" Dad asked suspiciously. "Is he, you know, doing okay?"

The old man didn't answer, but he rang up the groceries and the fishing rods without another word. Dad looked over at Ryan and gave him a look. *Told you. They think he's different around here.*

He is different, Ryan wanted to say, if it had been polite to tell the whole truth and nothing but the truth in front of a stranger.

The old man bagged everything quickly and took their father's money. He gave them all a quick once-over, a little wave of thanks, and turned to scurry back into the stock room. But Abby stopped him with a question before he could get behind the curtain.

The old man turned back to her. "What did you say?" His expression had changed. His eyes had hardened, and his brow pinched together in a frown.

She repeated her question. "What happened to all those people's pets? The ones in the posters?" She jutted her thumb in the general direction of the community board.

The old man swept up to her, and for one terrifying second Ryan thought he was going to lunge over the counter and grab his sister by the neck.

"Why don't you ask your uncle Silas!" he exclaimed, shaking a fist at her.

"Hey now!" Their dad stepped in front of Abby, who yipped like a frightened puppy and hid behind him. "There's no reason for that. My daughter was simply asking a question."

"The curse," the man spat, as if he hadn't heard their father at all.

"What are you talking about?" Dad asked. "What curse?"

The old man shook his head in disbelief. "You don't know nothin', do ya? The woods 'round here—they're not safe at night. Don't be takin' your young ones in there, sir. I seen wolves, and other things, and they'll eat whatever they can catch."

Dad scoffed. "Wolves? That's ridiculous. A wolf hasn't been seen in the Adirondacks since one was shot back in 2001."

"Ain't natural." The old man shook his head and tutted. "Ain't natural wolves, no sir. The ones I seen … they must have been …" The old man searched his memory, and what he apparently saw there caused him to shudder violently.

"I can't … I can't talk about it no more." The old man looked like he was on the verge of crying. For a second, Ryan thought he was going to collapse. His legs wobbled a little as he turned and left them without another word, shuffling off into the back storeroom while muttering incoherently to himself.

Dad looked around at Ryan and Abby.

"Well," he said, picking up his purchases and putting on a smile that seemed all wrong on his face. "You find all kinds in these quaint little towns."

"What do you think he meant by the wolves not being natural?" Ryan asked as they left the store and went back to their car.

"I have no idea," he said.

Abby stopped on the sidewalk next to the car, looking up at the sky. Clouds had drifted in, but they were the white, cottony kind, not the bruisers that brought last night's storms.

"Abby?" Dad asked. "Everything all right?"

She stared mutely at the sky, ignoring the question.

"Come on, Abby," Ryan said. "Get in. I'm anxious to see Uncle Silas."

Abby dragged her gaze from the sky and settled it on him. Her eyes were empty, as though she were rooting around in that little attic room of hers again.

"Wolves."

Ryan blinked at his sister. "What about them?"

"I saw them."

"You saw wolves?"

"Get in, you two!" their dad shouted from behind the wheel.

"When did you see wolves?"

"In my dream last night."

"Abby, it was a dream, nothing more. Lots of people dream of scary stuff like wolves. I once dreamt of a wombat that had snuck into my room and ..."

Abby cut him off. "They're here, Ryan. *She's* here. I feel her presence in this place."

"Who?"

"Get in already!" Their father laid on the horn. A young couple pushing a stroller nearby looked over at them and frowned.

"I'll tell you later," Abby whispered.

Chapter 10

THEIR DAD MADE the last turn of the journey onto a dirt road in even worse condition than the one they'd just left. They bounced their way along a rutted, weed-choked dirt lane, anticipation building as they neared Uncle Silas's cabin.

Ryan rolled down his window to get some fresh air. He took a deep breath of tangy balsam fir. Then he caught a different scent, one that wrinkled his nose and churned his gut. It was bitter and sharp, like a smoky, chemical scent. It reminded him of the time a warehouse had burned down in his hometown. He'd been just a little kid, but he remembered how the smoke had filled the air for hours, making his eyes water and his throat burn. It smelled the same, *almost*, as the woods did now.

What if Uncle Silas had been hurt—or killed—in a forest fire?

"Dad, can you drive faster?" he urged. "Why are you going so slow?"

"Want me to blow out a tire?" he replied, glancing at Ryan. "What's the matter?"

"Probably nothing, but please hurry anyway. I just want to see Uncle Silas."

Abby must have sensed what he was feeling, too.

"Ryan's right," she said earnestly. "Please hurry."

Chapter 11

AROUND THE NEXT bend was Uncle Silas's place. It was a small cabin, set back from the road, with four wood-framed windows, a porch with two rocking chairs, and a stone chimney poking up through the middle of the roof. Weeds and vines entangled themselves around the porch steps and squirmed up the pillars. Two massive birch trees in the front yard loomed over the place like bodyguards.

Maybe 'bodyguards' wasn't the right word, or else

they had taken some time off, because the house was in shambles. The windows had been shattered, and the front door blown off its hinges. It lay in splintery pieces on the porch. Even the little green shed behind the house was violated by whatever attacked Uncle Silas. Its door hung askew and was hanging by one hinge.

Because Silas was a man with a meticulous nature, who kept even the smallest workspace in his house neat and orderly, the untidy appearance of the cabin was a shock to behold.

His sister leaned forward to whisper in his ear: "Death's been here."

He couldn't argue with her.

The cabin wasn't deserted, however. Uniformed police officers from the local sheriff's department milled around the grounds, surveying the damage. A few officers entered and exited the cabin by ducking under the yellow crime scene tape crisscrossing the gaping front door. Two deputies clutched notepads and scribbled furiously as a third man, possibly the sheriff himself, stood beside them talking and pointing things out.

"Wait here," Dad said, getting out of the car.

"Where are you going?" Ryan asked.

"To find out what happened, of course."

Ryan couldn't believe it. Just a few weeks ago he'd been on the phone with his great uncle, making plans for taking his boat out on Black Rock Lake to catch some bluegill. There wasn't a hint that anything was wrong. Not a word was mentioned of any problems Uncle Silas was having.

He glanced at Abby. "What do you think?"

Abby started opening her door.

"Hey, what are you doing?"

"I want to see," she said.

"Dad said to stay here—"

"I want to see."

Abby slid out of the car and scurried up to Dad as he approached the Sheriff. Dad didn't seem to notice.

Or, if he did, he probably figured it was pointless to shoo her away. Abby would persist. When her mind was made up, that's just what she did.

Sighing, Ryan unbuckled his seatbelt and got out as well. He knew at this point that it'd be up to him to hold the leash on his sister.

The sheriff's back was turned to them. He was shouting orders to someone to bag some evidence in the cabin when he turned around at the sound of their footsteps.

The sheriff was tall and broad-shouldered. Standing well over six feet tall, he had a square jaw and a short, trimmed mustache. Sunlight glinted off the gold badge he wore on his chest. Ryan swallowed a hard lump in his throat. *The sheriff wouldn't be here if a serious crime hadn't been committed.*

"Hold on there," he said, holding up his hands. "No one's allowed on the premises. It's a crime scene."

"What's going on here?" Dad demanded.

"Where's Silas?"

The sheriff studied each of them in turn, his mind no doubt taking mental notes and assessing how and what to tell them. His demeanor relaxed, and he said quietly, "We're not exactly sure what happened. We're still investigating."

"Is he here?"

"No, the cabin's empty. It's been ransacked. Who might you be?"

"My name is Jack Martin, and those are my kids back there in the–" He frowned when he noticed us standing right behind him. "They were supposed to be waiting in the car. Anyway, these are my kids, Abby and Ryan."

"My name's Sheriff Callahan." He shook their dad's hand, then he shook Ryan's. Abby shifted behind her brother, not one for human contact with strangers. Sheriff Callahan offered her a smile, and she gave a little wave. It was the most cordial greeting he was going to get out of her.

"What do you think happened, Sheriff?"

Ryan was surprised his sister asked the sheriff a question. Usually she stood like a mute statue until strangers walked away. The odd cadence of her little voice made the other officers within earshot stop what they were doing and stare at her, as if they'd never seen a child before. In fact, she did look out of place here, surrounded by police cruisers, crime scene investigators, and the deep woods. A little girl with alabaster skin and eyes the color of a misty lake. Yet in those eyes burned intense scrutiny that was impossible to ignore.

"Like I told your father, Abby, we're still investigating," he answered.

"Any theories?" she asked.

Sheriff Callahan licked his lips. "It looks like your uncle was..." He rubbed the back of his neck uncomfortably as he searched for the right word to use with a child.

"Abducted?" she said.

"Yes." Sheriff Callahan conceded.

"Abducted," Abby said, as if she were in a spelling bee. "To take someone away by force or deception."

Sheriff Callahan raised his eyebrows in surprise. "Yeah. That's right."

"What makes you think he was abducted?" Dad asked.

"Well, we found some unusual clues." He gestured for them to follow him.

As they approached the front door, Ryan heard his dad gasp sharply. "What happened?" The door had been smashed to pieces. Only a few inches of wood remained hinged to the doorframe.

"Whoever, or *whatever*, did this had been very strong," explained the sheriff.

"Excuse me?" Dad said. *"Whatever?"*

Sheriff Callahan nodded. "I don't think a man did this. This door was blown out from the *inside*, as if something huge and enormous was already inside and just smashed its way out. We found splinters as far away as twenty feet from the cabin, which would've required amazing force. I know Silas very well, Mr. Martin. A nice man ... but not exactly a bodybuilder."

No one said a word as this new information sank in.

The sheriff continued. "See those marks in the grass over there?"

Abby and Ryan peered around their father to see where the sheriff was pointing. On the lawn leading away from the door was a swath of matted-down grass leading to the forest.

"Those are drag marks," Sheriff Callahan said. "I think that's where they might've taken Silas."

"Okay, if someone–or some*thing*–dragged him out of his cabin, how did it get *in*."

Came Abby's lilting voice: "Up."

They followed her gaze to the roofline. The chimney caught Ryan's eye first, but next to it was a small attic window. The glass had been smashed.

"Who would want to get in so badly that they'd go

through the attic?" Ryan asked her.

She didn't immediately reply, so he gave her a little poke on the arm. She looked at him and shrugged vaguely: *You expect me to know everything?*

"This investigation is ongoing," Sheriff Callahan assured us. "Don't worry, we'll explore all possible leads. We should know more very soon. Do you have a place in town to stay?"

"We were supposed to be staying here," said their dad with a sigh.

"Well, that won't be possible."

"I guess we can find a hotel and ..." Dad stopped in mid-sentence when he noticed Abby was missing. He turned around in circles, looking for her. "Where did she go?" he asked no one in particular.

Two deputies who'd been standing nearby looked at each other, dumbfounded. "I don't know," one of them admitted. "She was right here a second ago."

Ryan hadn't seen his sister disappear, either. Sometimes she was like a spectre, drifting from one space to another—here one minute, gone the next.

"I'll look for her," he said. If he didn't volunteer, his dad would have recruited him anyway. "Abby!" he called, walking around to the back of the cabin, the only place he could think of to go look. "Abby, where did you go?"

The last thing they needed today was another missing person. He didn't want to see his sister's solemn face staring out from the community bulletin board of missing cat and dog pictures.

As expected, he found her in the little patch of grass that served as Uncle Silas's backyard, standing by his garden, which was an overgrown explosion of redolent herbs and plants, all of them flowering at once in a mishmash of color. Abby stood crouched on the ground, inspecting something. Ryan approached slowly, not wanting to startle her. He could tell she was in one of her trances.

"What did you find, Abby?" he asked quietly.

Her eyes were glued to the object in her hand. It

looked like an X made out of two birch sticks about five inches long, bound together in the middle by a leather strap.

"It's a totem," she said at last, in a distant voice. "They're all around back here. Probably in the front, too. Dozens of them. Maybe hundreds."

"What does it mean?" Ryan noticed a quiver had snuck into his voice.

"Uncle Silas was afraid of something."

"What?"

"Something evil."

He backed up a step. "I think we should show Dad and the sheriff."

"They wouldn't understand."

"It's a clue. This is an investigation."

"The answers they're looking for aren't here."

"What do you mean? You said he was afraid of something."

She was silent.

"Do you understand what's at stake here?"

She swung around and glowered at him. "Of course, I do!"

"Then we should tell the sheriff."

Abby looked almost disappointed in him. "Not yet, Ryan. I need time to figure this all out."

"You mean figure out what took him?"

"Not what," she corrected. "*Who.* I need to learn who she is."

"She?" he blurted. "You think a woman busted down that door, ransacked the place, and dragged Uncle Silas away?"

Abby continued to stare at the totem, saying nothing, turning it over and over in her hands as if perplexed by the mystery of its existence.

He said, "Is it the dream you had last night?"

She shrugged. "I don't know yet."

Ryan folded his arms and waited for his sister to elaborate. He knew pushing her too hard could distress her and send her over the edge, but he was eager for answers.

"This isn't the only mystery we have to solve," she said cryptically.

"What do you mean?"

"We're being watched."

Ryan glanced around. There was no one in sight. All the policemen were still in the front. In fact, it felt pretty lonely back here. And quiet. Like the woods were asleep.

"I don't see—"

"In the trees behind me," she murmured. "Be very still. Don't frighten him."

Ryan scanned the dense trees and thickets that bordered the yard, seeing nothing but greenery and shadows. Then, a furtive movement caught his eye. A flash of white. A face peering out from behind a tree.

A boy amidst the trees watched them. His hair was so blond it was almost white and his skin was mottled and gray. He looked sick, possibly even wounded in some way. Ryan gave a little wave. Never hurts to be friendly to the locals, he thought, especially his uncle's neighbors. The boy might, in fact, know something about what happened here.

"Hello!" Ryan called out. "Come talk to us!"

The boy didn't return the wave or the greeting, instead darting off into the dark interior of the woods.

"Must be a neighbor's kid," Ryan commented.

"Maybe."

Suddenly they heard their father's voice calling their names.

"C'mon, let's go." Ryan tugged gently on Abby's arm. "We have to get back now."

Silently, Abby slid the totem into the waistband of her shorts and covered it with her shirt. She'd ponder its secrets later.

Chapter 12

≈

WHEN RYAN AND Abby rejoined the others, they found someone new had arrived on the scene.

She was a woman of about sixty, tall and thin, with a slender face and a friendly smile. Her skin shined like wax, and her long black hair, laced with gray, flowed over her shoulders and down her back. She wore an unusually heavy black scarf, which seemed out of place on this hot summer day.

She was talking to their father and the sheriff, her

hands dashing through the air like crazed little birds as she spoke. She stopped when she noticed Ryan and Abby coming around the corner.

Her dark, almond-shaped eyes reminded Ryan of Egyptian pharaoh hieroglyphs. They had an impenetrable quality that made him uneasy. Though she appeared pleasant enough, when she zeroed in on Abby, it was with a strange familiarity, almost as if she were trying to decide if she knew her or not.

Or if she were friend or foe.

Abby slowed, and for a moment he thought she was going to run away. The lady with the long black hair smiled at them both, and the rows of teeth she revealed were perfectly straight and white. Her eyes, however, remained dark and inscrutable.

Their dad waved them forward. "You two shouldn't go wandering off like that."

The sheriff's tone was a lot less tolerant. "This is a crime scene now. You might have unknowingly trampled on evidence."

Ryan thought of the totem stuffed in Abby's pocket. *If you only knew.* "Sorry," he said. He glanced at his sister. Abby was staring at the woman as though she were a particularly complicated code she couldn't crack. Her brow furrowed and her mouth tightened.

Their dad introduced the stranger to them. "This is Mrs. Witheridge. She's a friend of your uncle's and lives up the road. She's willing to take us in while we search for your uncle."

"You mean we can help you find Uncle Silas?" Ryan asked the sheriff.

The sheriff shook his head. "Stay with your sister, son. Watch out for her," he said. Ryan nodded unhappily. He might as well be wearing a t-shirt that said ABBY'S PERSONAL BODYGUARD on it.

"It's okay, Ryan. I'm sure he won't be missing for long." Mrs. Witheridge said, extending a hand to him in greeting. Each fingernail was lacquered in black nail polish. *Sharp as razors*, he noticed. He stepped forward and shook her hand gingerly. He expected it to feel like a loose bundle of sticks wrapped in dry linen, but there was remarkable strength in her grasp. In fact, her squeeze made him wince a little bit.

"I've known Silas for years," she said in a warm tone. "Such a kindly man, always willing to help an old widow like me when she needs it."

"Thank you."

"I'll make you all comfortable in my home, Ryan. I have a lovely little cottage, with a beautiful view of the lake. There's a dock you can dive off, and the fishing is excellent." She winked when he smiled.

"That sounds like fun," he said.

"Excellent! And who do we have here?" Mrs. Witheridge turned her smile up to full wattage and clapped her hands.

In typical fashion, Abby shrank into herself and put her head down shyly.

"Uh, this is Abby," Dad said. "She doesn't take to strangers much at first, but she'll warm up."

Mrs. Witheridge beamed. "I'm sure she'll warm to

oatmeal cookies in no time." She crouched down to talk to Abby face to face. "Do you like s'mores, honey? You see, I have a fire pit in my backyard, and we could get a nice bonfire going tonight and roast marshmallows and tell campfire stories. Do you like stories?"

"Yes," she murmured.

"What is your favorite kind of story?"

Almost in a whisper, "I'll read anything."

"Really? A little scholar."

Abby straightened and recited in a strong, clear voice: "Scholar. A distinguished academic, particularly in the humanities!"

Mrs. Witheridge studied Abby with curious fascination. Surprisingly, her smile didn't falter. Most people who encountered Abby for the first time sensed her oddness immediately and reacted with thinly disguised contempt, even going so far as to back away warily or make up a reason to excuse themselves. They acted as though they might catch a disease if they stood too close to her. *If they had even one-tenth of Abby's intelligence or uncanny abilities, they would be better for it,* Ryan thought. Too bad most people were too foolish to realize that.

Mrs. Witheridge, however, didn't look at Abby like that. She seemed in awe of her. Yet the skeptical part of his brain told him to be suspicious of anyone who didn't react without *some* disbelief toward Abby.

As if sensing she'd been staring too long at Abby, Mrs. Witheridge stood up and turned toward Dad. "Well, Mr. Martin, should we proceed to my place? The afternoon light isn't long for us now and we should really get you and your family settled in before dark."

Dad nodded appreciatively. "Sounds good." He glanced at Sheriff Callahan, who hitched his thumbs in his gun belt. "Will you let me know as soon as you find anything, Sheriff?"

"I can do you one better," he replied. "We're forming a search party right now as we speak. We'll be heading out as soon as we're through with our investigation here. You're welcome to join us."

"I'd like that."

Sheriff Callahan nodded. "Things like this don't happen here in Black Rock Falls, Mr. Martin. We're a small town of nice folks ... but these woods." He paused, glancing around as though suddenly worried about being watched. "They can be dangerous. No one knows that better than your uncle."

"Dangerous, how?"

"Come on," interrupted Mrs. Witheridge. She gently led Ryan, Abby and their father back to their car. "Let's get you settled in first. There'll be time for talk later."

Chapter 13

HEY FOLLOWED Mrs. Witheridge through a rusted gate and up a red stone pathway to her cottage. The cottage was neat and inviting, painted blue and white, with landscaped flower beds and bird baths dotting the front yard.

She unlocked the back door and led them inside. The kitchen was enormous, dominated by a long pinewood table in the middle. Abby immediately noticed the pleasant fragrances lingering in the air. On the kitchen counter was a small mound of dried lavender. Next to it sat a basket of spices, and beside it, a cup of pure black liquid that she recognized immediately as licorice-infused oil.

"I make soaps and candles," Mrs. Witheridge explained, noticing the curiosity on Abby's face. "I have a small but loyal clientele. Doesn't pay much but it helps me get by."

She took them on a tour of the rest of the house. Heavy damask draperies hung in the living rooms. In the dim light Abby saw bookshelves lined with row after row of gleaming leather-bound books. In fact, books and newspapers lay everywhere, covering the furniture and the surfaces of the coffee and side tables. A hand-carved sign on the wall next to the window read: A House is not a Home unless it contains food and fire for the mind as well as the body.

Abby read the sign aloud. "Benjamin Franklin," she stated at the end.

Mrs. Witheridge gazed at her admiringly. "Remarkable. Yes, he is the one who said it. Do you agree with Mr. Franklin's definition of a home?"

Abby nodded enthusiastically.

Mrs. Witheridge showed Ryan and Abby to the guest room where they'd be sleeping. It was a small, tidy guestroom with a single bed, nightstand, and a tall cherrywood bureau for clothes in the corner. Mrs. Witheridge told them she'd bring in a cot so they wouldn't have to share the bed.

"What about the room across the hall?" Abby inquired.

Mrs. Witheridge's eyebrow arched. "What about it?"

"You didn't show it to us."

"Abby," her father snapped, "you know better. That was rude."

"Not at all, Mr. Martin," said Mrs. Witheridge pleasantly. "She has a probing mind; I like that about her. The room, my dear, is my private study. I like my solitude, which is the main reason I live alone. If you thought the living room was messy, you should see where I do my real work!"

"You mean you make soap and candles in there, too?" asked Ryan.

Mrs. Witheridge eyes sparkled with amusement. "No, my boy. My real job is something much different."

Before anyone could pester their host anymore, their father told them to start unpacking. "You have a lovely home," he said as he walked out with her. "How long have you known Silas?"

Abby and Ryan listened as their voices faded down the hall, then Abby shut the door quietly.

"What do you think?" Ryan asked her.

"About what?"

"What do you mean, 'about what'? About Mrs. Witheridge. She seems nice enough."

"She's hiding something."

"You mean, in her study?"

"Not just there. There's more to her than we see on the surface."

"Isn't that the case with everybody?"

Abby looked at her brother with astonishment. "That's deep coming from you, Ryan."

"Hey, I'm not just a big dumb jock."

Abby grinned. "I know. You're not that big."

Ryan threw a pillow at her and then went about unpacking his bags. Abby went over to the bed and pulled the totem out of her waistband, examining it closely and running her fingers over the strange symbols and slash marks carved into it.

She shook her head uncertainly. "Definitely afraid of something," she muttered under her breath. She slipped it under her pillow for safekeeping.

Dad came back a few minutes later and told them to wash up because Mrs. Witheridge was serving dinner soon. When they went to the kitchen, they found the table set with bowls of fresh fruit and plates of sandwiches. A vase of brightly colored flowers sat in the middle.

They sat down and started eating. After a short while filled with pleasant small talk, Abby said, "You told us you live alone."

"I do. Ever since my husband passed away a few years back."

"Then why do you lock the door?"

For a moment her smile faltered. "What door are you referring to, dear?"

"The one at the end of the hall, across from our room."

Mrs. Witheridge laughed, but it sounded forced to Abby. "As I've said before, that's the door to my office, and it's a very personal space to me. I keep it locked all the time. I have important papers in there, and all the research I've done for my book."

"You're writing a book?" she asked.

"I am."

"What's it about?"

"Legends of the Adirondack mountains. Folklore. Local superstition."

"Our dad writes books like that," she pointed out. Dad nodded sheepishly.

Mrs. Witheridge eyes widened in surprise. "Does he, now? I'm the town historian. There are many stories that people outside of the Adirondacks have never heard before, and I want to put them together into one book. A kind of testimony to the wisdom of the rugged folks who call the mountains home."

"Can you tell us a story now?"

Mrs. Witheridge knitted her eyebrows in thought. "You really want to hear one?"

Abby nodded eagerly.

"All right, then." Mrs. Witheridge settled black in her chair and clasped her hands on her lap. "I'll tell you one. But you must sign an affidavit stating you won't divulge any details about the book until it's published, or my agent will be very upset." She winked playfully at Abby.

"Don't worry. Your secret is safe with me."

Mrs. Witheridge smiled cleverly at the girl. "I'll bet you keep many secrets."

Abby's cheeks turned a bright pink.

"I'm sorry if I've embarrassed you."

Abby shrugged. "Don't worry about it. You're right, though—I do keep secrets. If I told them … no one would believe me anyway."

"Your brother would."

Maybe, Abby thought. After all he'd been through the last two days, and all that he'd learned about Uncle Silas and himself, Ryan's mind had been opened in ways even he didn't realize yet.

"Well," Mrs. Witheridge began, quickly changing the subject back to her book. "One of the earliest industries in the Adirondack region was logging, for obvious reasons. There was and still is today a wealth of lumber—pine, oak, beech, maple, and birch, to name just a few—and loggers would work tirelessly to clear the forests and make a few men very, very rich."

"I can't believe anybody would want to cut down such a beautiful place like this," Abby said.

"There were new settlements moving in all the time," Mrs. Witheridge explained, "and so lumber was in very high demand. In any case, because they were too heavy to move over land, logs were transported down rivers to the sawmills. There were times when the Saranac was chocked full of so many logs, you could practically walk across them like a bridge to the other side."

Their father nodded in agreement.

"Well, one day, a boy not much older than you tried to do just that. He tried to cross the Saranac on the backs of those rolling logs. His name was Thomas Strauss. His friends didn't think he should do it, but the boy was proud and wanted to show off his courage.

"At dusk, his friends watched as Tom started across the river, picking his spots carefully as he stepped from one log to the next. He was half-way across when his friends started cheering him on to go faster. The boy, obviously excited, turned back to wave at his friends. But as soon as he took his eyes off the logs, one rolled under him and he pitched forward, falling into the river.

"His friends could do nothing but watch and pray as they waited for some sign from the boy that he was all right. You see, the logs were bunched together so tightly, the other boys had no idea where exactly Tom fell in. They waited. It must have felt like an eternity. They waited to see Tom stick an arm up in the air, call for help, *anything* to let them know he was still alive. But there was no sign of him; he never resurfaced.

"The logs continued their journey downstream, dragging Tom's body with them. It wasn't long after that when people began reporting strange sounds and seeing ghostly white figures of a young boy hovering over the river. They say to this day that Tom still haunts the Saranac River, and you can catch a glimpse of him on moonless nights, right around dusk, standing in the middle of the rushing water, waving to friends on the shore."

Nobody said anything. A clock in the corner ticked the seconds by as they each absorbed the story Mrs.

Witheridge had told. Then Dad cleared his throat and announced he had to be going. He was itching to get out and help with the search.

Abby got visibly agitated, fidgeting in her seat and staring at her untouched plate.

"Any idea where you're going to be looking for Silas?" Mrs. Witheridge asked their father.

"Some folks apparently saw him hiking from time to time up to a place called Sutter's Hill," said Dad. "I overheard a couple of the deputies talking about it. Could be a connection of some kind."

"I thought he was abducted," Ryan said, perplexed. "You're making it sound like he just went out for a stroll and got lost."

"It's called hope, Ryan," Dad answered, standing up from the table with a heavy sigh. "I should get going. I don't know when I'll be back."

He leaned over and gave Abby a kiss on the forehead. "Your uncle will be okay. He's been taking care of himself in these woods for over forty years.

Things have a way of working themselves out for the best, if you keep a positive outlook."

Ryan didn't feel positive about anything at that moment, but he was relieved when his sister gave their dad a little smile.

He said to Ryan, "Take care of your sister. I don't have any bars on my cellphone, so I won't be able to call."

"We're pretty much cut off from the rest of the world out here," Mrs. Witheridge said. "Like the first pioneers to settle this land."

Pretty much? Ryan almost laughed. It felt like they'd been time-warped back to the eighteenth century.

After Dad left, they picked at the rest of their dinner in silence. Ryan's food sat at the bottom of his stomach like a stone, hardened by dread over what may have happened to Uncle Silas.

"I know you can't help worrying," Mrs. Witheridge told him when she noticed him push his plate away, "but Sheriff Callahan will get him back. He's a good man. He's lived here all his life and knows these woods as well as anyone. If anyone can find him, he can."

"What if he can't?" Abby asked in a small voice.

"Sheriff Callahan will do all he can to track him down and get him back."

Ryan leaned forward. "Who would want to do this to Uncle Silas?"

Mrs. Witheridge held her hands apart. "Who knows why people do the things they do? Of course, not everybody liked your uncle. Some folks accused of him doing witchy things up at his cabin."

The air in the room felt like it dropped ten degrees in a matter of seconds.

"Mrs. Witheridge," Abby said, "what 'witchy things' are you talking about?"

Their host dabbed the corners of her mouth with her napkin before answering. "Some folks around here are afraid of your uncle. Others revere him. He's helped many people over the years and does it for next to nothing. I don't know how he survives."

"What's 'witchy' about that?" she persisted.

"A long time ago, people like your uncle were called cunning folk. Shamans. *Witches.* You see, your uncle heals people with homegrown remedies. He makes potions and medicines by hand, as native cultures have been doing for thousands of years. He has a rare gift, and people around here know that, but—"

"But not everyone is okay with it," Ryan finished for her.

"There are always unsatisfied customers," she continued. "And, naturally, the more power you have, the more folks are going to fear you. A lot of people are afraid of Silas because they don't understand him. They think ... well, it's quite foolish, actually."

Mrs. Witheridge lapsed into silence and stared into her coffee cup, lost in thought.

"What's foolish?" Ryan prompted.

"The notion some people have around here that because your uncle has a natural gift for healing, he must have acquired it from … devious sources."

"He's not like that!" Abby shot up from the table, knocking her chair over. "Why do people have to be so mean and ignorant? Why can't they leave us alone?" She ran out of the room, her teary sobs growing fainter as she retreated to the guestroom and slammed the door.

"Sorry about that," Ryan said ruefully. He was used to making excuses on behalf of his sister's unpredictable behavior.

"I'm sorry too," Mrs. Witheridge replied, setting the chair back in place. "I didn't mean to upset her."

"Don't worry about it. These days it doesn't take much to set her off."

After a few seconds of listening to her muffled cries float down the hallway, Mrs. Witheridge asked, "Would you like any dessert? I have a pecan pie we can cut into."

Ryan shook his head and patted his stomach. "No, thanks. Maybe later? I feel like I ate a horse."

"You wouldn't be the first one around here to do that," she said, clearing the table.

When she noticed Ryan's surprise, her eyes twinkled with amusement. "You don't believe me? In the early colonial days, it was hard to survive in the wilderness. When the first settlers arrived here, they found harsh conditions—forests that needed clearing, unfriendly natives, and brutal winters. Some people quit and went south for warmer climates or returned to England. Many early settlers died during those long winters."

"What made them stay?"

Mrs. Witheridge shrugged. "Oh, a lot of things, I guess. Even when there is plenty of danger, some people don't know when to quit. They persist, even when there are obvious signs they should back down."

"Maybe they just liked the taste of horse meat?"

"They ate whatever they could to survive."

Ryan thought about that. He couldn't imagine not having all the conveniences of a modern life. With death always so near, it was no wonder people back then were superstitious.

"I should check on Abby," he said. But before he left the kitchen, he turned back to Mrs. Witheridge. A question had been nagging him since they left Uncle Silas's cabin.

"Are there ghosts in these woods?"

Mrs. Witheridge turned from the sink where she was washing dishes and stared at him. A thin smile stretched her lips. "Ghosts? Did my story get to you that much?"

"No," he said, "it's just something the sheriff said. The police have no idea how someone—or some*thing*, as he put it—got into his place. And the cabin … it was all torn up inside and out. What could have had that sort of power?"

"I don't have the answer to that. But I can tell you that ghosts don't attack people and tear up their houses."

"I know," he said, feeling foolish. "I don't believe

in that stuff, but Abby thinks all of it is real. She knows a lot about the supernatural."

"Does she?" Mrs. Witheridge looked intrigued. "Listen, Ryan. There are places in the forest that nobody has ever been. Dark corners where almost anything can be lurking. But I can tell you one thing: in all my years living in these mountains, no one has ever been attacked by anything 'out of this world'."

He smiled. What a silly conversation to be having. Yet he couldn't deny feeling better after hearing Mrs. Witheridge say those encouraging words.

Chapter 14

"WHAT'S WRONG with you?" Ryan asked his sister a few minutes later, fully realizing it was a loaded question. He found her lying on the bed in the dark, staring up at the ceiling in a deep meditative state.

Last time he'd seen her like that, she didn't speak to anyone for a week, even her teachers. When she came out of it, her only excuse was, "Something was on my mind." When pressed to explain what was bothering her, the only thing she would say was,

"Behind the garage, under the wheelbarrow, next to the hose." No one had any idea what she meant.

But then five days later their neighbor showed up on their back doorstep, apologizing profusely for what he called "the accident." His dog, a rottweiler named Tank, had killed their cat Whiskers.

Their neighbor found the mangled cat's body behind the garage. Under the wheelbarrow. Next to the hose.

"Are you all right, Abs?" When she didn't answer at first, he repeated, "Abby?"

"Do you smell it?" Abby took a deep sniff of the air. "It's there ... lingering."

"Smell what?" He shrugged. The room, like the rest of the cottage, was lightly fragranced with the scents of spices and herbs, presumably from Mrs. Witheridge's soap-and-candle-making business. But there was nothing else peculiar beyond that. "I don't smell anything."

"It's gone." Abby said now, shaking her head

uncertainly. "I thought I smelled … magic."

"And what exactly does *magic* smell like?"

"Like rain," she said. "The good kind."

"The good kind of rain?"

She glanced at him and frowned. "The good kind of magic. You smelled the other earlier today in the forest."

"I think you're imagining things," he said, not wanting to let on that he knew what she was talking about. The bitter, burning scent on the drive up the dirt road to the cabin. Like sulfur.

She didn't answer. Instead, she swung her legs out of bed and crept up to the door.

"Where are you going?"

"I want to see the room across the hall."

"You know we can't go in there."

"I'm just curious."

Ryan wouldn't admit it to Abby, but he wanted to see what was inside the room, too. But defying Mrs. Witheridge and making her angry didn't seem like a smart move. Though she was just a thin wisp of a woman with about as much substance to her as a milkweed plant, there was a force to her presence that suggested a deep well of strength. Maybe not the physical kind, but he'd seen enough of Abby's own *force* to know how unpredictable certain people can be.

"I need to see inside that room!" Abby insisted. He hated it when she pouted.

"Forget it, Abs. It's probably locked."

"I can open it."

"How?"

She looked up at him and smiled cleverly. "With *this*." She slid a hair pin out of her pocket. "I keep one handy just in case."

"In case of what? You get the urge to commit a misdemeanor?" Ryan didn't like where this was going. It was one thing to sneak into his room in the middle of the night and involve him in paranormal parlor tricks. But it was wrong to break into somebody else's private space. He was about to explain the difference to Abby when she slipped out the door and pattered across the hall.

"Abby, come back here!" He caught her in time before she had a chance to pick the lock and dragged her back into their room. "What's wrong with you? We can't go around doing what we please in other people's houses."

"Did you see Mrs. Witheridge's reaction when Dad mentioned Sutter's Hill? It was like she was scared of something."

"Big deal."

"She looked like she'd seen a ghost."

"So? Maybe she knows someone who died there."

"Exactly." Abby nodded. "We need to find out all we can about this place—and Mrs. Witheridge—if we're going to have any chance of finding Uncle Silas."

"You think she's connected somehow to his disappearance?"

Abby nodded. "I know it."

"The police are looking for him," Ryan replied,

shaking his head, "and they told us to stay put."

"They won't find him."

"How do you know?"

"He's someplace … *else*."

He watched her face go blank and her eyes widen, as though her attic door had sprung open and a revelation tumbled out.

"What are you sensing, Abby?"

"We need to know what's behind that door," she said with a tone of finality.

"Another forecast?" he asked.

She swayed, suddenly, like she was going to faint, and her eyes rolled up into the back of her head. "Catch me, Ryan," she murmured, and pitched forward into his arms.

Alarmed, he carried her back to bed. Her skin had gone pale, and a cold sweat broke out over her body. Her chest shuddered, as if it took effort to breathe. Then she bent her head backwards and twisted it side to side, her eyes staring wildly up at the ceiling, a silver thread of saliva leaking from the corner of her slack mouth. This was more than a trance, Ryan realized with horror; this was some sort of seizure! He called for Mrs. Witheridge as he supported Abby's head in the crook of his arm. Groans escaped her throat, followed by grunts that formed bits and pieces of nonsensical words. Swiftly, her hands flew up to her face, and she waved them all around, as if brushing an irritating mosquito away.

His heart pounded. *She's going to die, and I'm going to be blamed for it. I let Abby down. I'm supposed to protect her!*

"Mrs. Witheridge!" he screamed again, and then Abby's seizure stopped as quickly as it had started. Abby blinked twice, and the clouds cleared from her eyes. Her face relaxed, no longer squeezed

in the vice-grip of terror. A light pink color returned to her cheeks.

She looked up at him. "He's nearby," she intoned, "but so is *she.*"

She abruptly wiped her mouth and yanked the

covers up to her chin, curling up and closing her eyes.

"Who, Abby?" he asked desperately. Her speedy recovery unnerved him as much as her sudden attack, and part of him was afraid it would start all over again. "What are you talking about? *Who's* near?"

"I need to sleep."

"You can't leave me hanging like this, Abs."

"Good night."

"Wait!"

But she was gone, fast asleep.

Chapter 15

MRS. WITHERIDGE appeared at the door.

"Is everything all right? I heard my name and—" She stopped when she saw Abby sleeping as stiff as a board on the bed. Her lips pursed together. "What happened?"

"Abby had a seizure of some kind, just freaked out on me. She's never done that before."

Mrs. Witheridge nodded as if she saw this sort of thing all the time. She came over and lightly touched Abby's forehead. "No fever," she said, sounding satisfied. She stroked Abby's long blond hair.

"Is she okay?"

Mrs. Witheridge looked at Ryan and smiled. "I think she is now, but I want to be sure."

"Should we call a doctor or an ambulance or something?"

"If I had a phone, it would be a possibility," she reminded him calmly. "I'm pretty much off the grid here, as they say."

Ryan felt uneasy. He hadn't had a bar pop up on his own cell phone since they'd arrived at Black Rock Falls. "How do you get help if you need it?"

"I have other ways." She touched his shoulder reassuringly as she turned to leave the room.

"Where are you going?"

"I'll be right back."

Ryan watched his sister sleep while he waited. Her steady, rhythmic breathing was the only sound in the room save for the ticking of a small clock on the bureau. Twice he felt her forehead for a fever, but she seemed okay. He was no doctor, of course. For that matter, neither was Mrs. Witheridge. He wished Dad would get back soon. Ryan felt suddenly lonely and vulnerable in the little cottage.

And on top of it all, he felt *watched*, though he couldn't explain why. It was as though an unseen presence shared the room with him.

Mrs. Witheridge returned a minute later carrying an armload of candles, vials and containers. She laid them out on the nightstand next to the bed, placing the three black candles in the middle.

"What's all that for?" Ryan wondered aloud.

Mrs. Witheridge struck a match and lit the three candles, murmuring words he couldn't quite catch. Then she handed him an empty plastic cup.

"Go out in my yard and quickly fill this with soil. You'll find a shovel in the shed."

"What for?"

Mrs. Witheridge leveled her gaze at him. "Don't ask questions. All will be revealed to you soon enough.

Just do what I ask."

Reluctant to leave his sister alone with someone he'd only just met that day, Ryan stood by the bed, staring at the cup.

"*Go,*" she ordered him, "if you want to see your sister protected from harm."

Against his better judgment, he shuffled out of the room. He was used to Abby's eccentric behavior, but he didn't think Mrs. Witheridge would be as odd. Maybe he'd judged her too soon.

Now that night had fallen and cast its spell of shadows across the land, the sense of an unseen presence was back, watching him as he went outside. He found a small shovel in the shed and dug a scoop of dirt out of the ground. Was he supposed to pick the grass out of it before he brought it inside? She didn't say. What would Abby expect? She probably wouldn't want the grass, so he plucked it out and crumbled the damp soil into the cup.

Satisfied he had enough, he started back into the

house when a scuffling sound in the woods behind him made him stop. He turned around and squinted into the blackness. All he saw were crowded trees, standing at attention, tall and silent. There was no wind on this chilly night. Dew beads gleamed like opals in the pale moonlight.

Get moving.

He took that advice from the part of his brain in charge of his physical well-being and crossed the tiny yard to the cottage in seven quick strides. As his hand reached for the door, a howl stopped him short.

Wolves. More than one. Maybe several.

Wolves in the Adirondacks? he thought. *Didn't his dad say there weren't any around here?*

He saw their eyes peering out at him in the woods, chips of glassy light pacing back and forth, waiting. If they had wanted to, Ryan knew they could have attacked him—even killed him—or dragged him off to wherever Uncle Silas was taken. Why were they just watching? What did they want?

One member of the pack howled again, and the others joined in, making a chorus of bone-chilling bays and yowls that echoed across the mountains.

Ryan dashed inside, slammed the back door shut, and threw his weight against it. The air inside the cottage felt stifling and hot compared to outside, but at least in here he was safe. He waited for his heart to stop jabbing his rib cage before going to see Mrs. Witheridge.

He found her just as he had left her, hunched over Abby, doting. He gave her the cup of soil and stood back, wondering what would come next.

"What's the empty wine bottle for?" he asked. While he was outside, Mrs. Witheridge had opened the jars and vials and laid out the ingredients on a sheet on the floor. There were herbs that he recognized from his own parents' garden: basil, dill, juniper, and tarragon. A stick of dried sage. Garlic cloves and three bay leaves. A few tiny, brown, rose thorns. A smooth, black gemstone that looked like onyx. And, finally, a plastic container of sharp objects like nails and sewing needles.

"I'm casting a protective spell," Mrs. Witheridge told him, never taking her eyes off Abby.

"You're *what*?"

"I know this is hard for you to understand, but don't ignore what's right in front of you." She gave him a sympathetic look. "You've learned a lot from your sister; you just don't want to admit it to yourself. And your Uncle Silas ... you know who he is. *Cunning folk*. You need to listen to Abby and me and do exactly what we say... and *believe* ... if you want to see your sister survive the next two nights."

"What are you talking about?"

"If you don't know, then you haven't been listening."

Ryan was speechless. If Abby's life was in danger in any way, and Mrs. Witheridge could help her, then he'd do anything she told him to.

Apparently satisfied he wouldn't be asking any

more questions, Mrs. Witheridge turned her attention back to Abby. She touched her cheek tenderly and whispered words that floated on the air like smoke, and then set about making the witch bottle.

First, she lit the three black candles. Next, she took the cup of soil Ryan had dug up in the back yard and poured it into the bottle. As she did this, she recited:

> *"Protective spirits, attend my work,*
> *and add your power to mine.*
> *Cast your light upon this child,*
> *and grant her protection divine."*

When she was done saying the spell, she poured more of the ingredients into the witch bottle: the onyx, garlic, and rose thorns. She gave the bottle a gentle shake and then added the rest to the mix: the bay leaves, the sharp metal objects, and the other herbs. Finally, she uncorked a vial of vinegar and poured it into the bottle, too. When she was done, she sealed the bottle with melting wax from a candle, and said these words:

> *"Protective spirits, honor my work;*
> *your power has been joined with mine.*
> *Keep this child safe from evil*
> *and grant her protection divine."*

She closed her eyes and recited the incantation three more times. When she finished, she set the bottle down on the nightstand, blew out the candles, and gathered up all her materials. Arms full, she swept past Ryan and headed for the door.

"She needs to rest now," she said over her shoulder.

"Is she okay?"

"I believe she will be. Don't worry, Ryan. Let the magic have a chance to take effect." With that, she closed the bedroom door with a soft click.

Interlude 2
What he learns in the dark

Down in the dark, the old man waits. He senses the witch's vile presence all around him, like a suffocating stench, and knows she is biding her time. He hopes death will be merciful and that she will spare him the worst of the pain ... but he holds out little hope.

She will, no doubt, take great pleasure in her work, and make him suffer an eternity's worth of agony.

He tries to get a message out to Abby, his niece, whom he senses is very close by, to stay away and go back home. His mind meets a wall of resistance, which, try as he might, he is unable to penetrate. In essence, he's knocked on the door of her subconscious, but his voice and his words cannot be heard.

He knows the source of the resistance. Its ghastly, shriveled human form lurches about in the cabin upstairs, cackling mirthlessly to itself. If Abby doesn't get away from here soon, it is only a matter of time before the witch gets her, too. He wishes he had more time to teach her. There is still so much to tell and show her about their true natures. She is the best kind of student—willing and eager, bright and devoted—and if given enough time to develop her powers … oh, what a formidable foe she could be!

Yet time is running out. The blood moon will be rising soon. Then the witch will make Abby pay for a centuries-old covenant. Part of Silas resents his bloodline. It is unfair to place a burden like this on anyone against their will, especially a child.

Yet the deed is done. And, at the time, it was no doubt a wise choice. Would he have done anything different if he'd witnessed the horrors of Salem Village in 1692?

Probably not.

David R. Smith

Silas keeps an ear tuned to the movements up above, noting every scrape of a chair, swish of a broom, or scurry of an animal. He forms a mental map of what the floorplan up above must look like, in the hope he will need it to escape.

As he imagines the layout of the cabin above for the thousandth time, a scream of torment breaks the silence. Heavy footsteps thud on the floorboards overhead, causing dust and grit to rain down on his head. The cellar door groans open and the thing comes rushing down the stairs, stealthy as a cat, and glares at him in the shaft of light with blood-red eyes.

"I want her, Silas!" demands the witch, her voice raspy.

"Who?" the old man croaks.

"Don't play games with me." The thing scuttles over like a spider to where he lies on the filthy ground and kneels over him, the stink of her breath making him gag.

"I want the girl," it whispers darkly. "I saw her, in my visions. I want access to her mind—give it to me!"

"I can no more give you another's mind as I can give you another's soul."

"She is your kin, old man. You have taught her the old

ways. You can open the door."

"Why don't you ask your master?" he says defiantly. *"Perhaps he has not gifted you with as much power as you thought for your loyalties."*

The thing recoils, its lips peeling back in a feral smile. "I will kill you soon, old man, and when I do, it will be a thousand times the agony of my persecuted sisters at the hands of those hypocrite Puritans. But not yet. When the blood moon rises tomorrow night, and my powers are ready, I will lift this curse once and for all and be free."

God help us, *Silas thinks.*

Chapter 16

YAN STIRRED IN bed. When he opened his eyes, he was surprised to find it was already morning. He'd meant to lie down on the cot and wait for Abby to wake up, but he must have been more exhausted than he thought.

Even more surprising was the fact that Abby was sitting up in bed, reading a familiar hardcover book: *A Supernatural History of the World*. He didn't realize she'd brought it with her from home.

"Oh, hello," she said brightly, when she noticed

him staring at her. "How did you sleep?"

"Fine." He yawned. "How long have you been awake?"

"A couple hours now."

He was stunned. "Why didn't you tell me?"

"I couldn't. You were sleeping. Did you know you snore?"

"Abby! I was worried sick about you last night!"

"No need … I'm fine. But you should listen to this. I'm learning something very interesting.

"'Abigail Williams was born on July 12, 1680 in Salem, Massachusetts,'" she read from the book. "'She lived with her uncle, Reverend Samuel Parris, his daughter Betty Paris, and their slave Tituba."

"That's great," Ryan interrupted, "but I'm really not in the mood for a history less…"

"'In January of 1692, Abigail and Betty began acting strangely. They would throw fits, scream for no apparent reason, and claim spirits were pinching and harassing them. This started, some say, after Tituba taught the girls about a fortune-telling technique called the Venus-glass.

"'By the end of February, Reverend Parris had called a doctor to examine the girls, who were not getting any better. Perplexed, the doctor could find no medical reason for their physical condition, and declared the girls bewitched. Three days later, Abigail and Betty named their tormentors: Tituba, Sara Osborne, and Sara Goode. In March, the three women stood trial on charges of witchcraft.

"'At trial, Tituba confessed to witchcraft, and warned that many more witches roamed the village of Salem. This sparked the hysteria that would see over two hundred people accused of witchcraft and twenty of them executed. Records show that Abigail Williams herself accused fifty-seven people of witchcraft. This was one of the darkest times in human history.'"

Ryan lay back on the cot when she finished reciting the text. "Why are you telling me this? What does it have to do with Uncle Silas's disappearance?"

"I'm not sure yet, but I have a hunch."

"A hunch. Do you even know what that means?" He immediately regretted asking the question.

"Hunch. A feeling or guess based on intuition rather than known facts!"

"Thank you, Miss Dictionary." He rolled over and closed his eyes. His head ached from too little sleep. Now that he knew Abby was okay, maybe he could catch a few more winks. It was too early in the morning for talk of witches or cryptic Abby-isms.

Just as he was drifting off to sleep again, a loud thump woke him up. Abby had dropped the book on the floor next to his head. "Wake up!" she cried. "We have work to do."

"Whu—what?"

"We're going exploring."

He sat up again and rubbed his bleary eyes. "Now hold on—"

"You want to get to the bottom of all this, don't you?"

"How are we going to do that?"

"I think the answer might be found in Uncle Silas's cabin."

"You heard what Dad said."

"I didn't hear Dad say anything," she replied in her infuriatingly smug way.

"Oh, no? About not hiking too far? Staying close to the cottage?"

"Uncle Silas only lives a little way up the road. It's not that far at all."

"I don't think that's what Dad meant."

She frowned at him. "We can't sit around all day doing nothing!"

"It could be dangerous."

A cunning smile crossed her lips. "You're not afraid, are you, big brother?"

He bristled. "Of course not!"

"Then why don't you want to see what happened at the cabin? There could be clues."

"The police would have found them by now."

She rolled her eyes. "I'm not talking about *those* kinds of clues."

Of course, she meant *magical* clues. The sort you could divine in a scrying bowl.

"What are you going to do once we get there?"

"There's something we need to find."

"Clues, you mean."

"No, more than that. Something for Mom."

Ryan's heart skipped a beat. What did any of this have to do with their mother?

"What could Mom possibly need in Uncle Silas's cabin."

"I don't have time to explain now."

"Sure, you do."

"I'll explain on the way. First, let's eat. I smell bacon."

In fact, bacon was cooking in the kitchen when they got there. So were pancakes and sausages. Ryan watched his sister eat with a gusto that wasn't like her usual nit-picking and complaining. True, she added enough salt to her food to harden a horse's arteries, but that only meant she was in a good mood.

An Abby mood.

A let's-face-the-day-and-turn-it-weird mood.

When they finished, Abby and Ryan helped Mrs. Witheridge do the dishes and then announced they were going for a walk.

"Are you feeling better so soon?" Mrs. Witheridge asked Abby, eyeing her skeptically.

"Oh, yes," she responded matter-of-factly. "Maladies hit me hard from time to time, but they never last."

Mrs. Witheridge cocked an eyebrow. "You are unique, Abby. But I guess you already know that."

"Unique!" Abby stuck her pointer finger up in the air like a lecturing professor. "Being the only one of its kind; unlike anything else!"

"Yep," Ryan agreed. "That's you."

Mrs. Witheridge walked them to the door. "Just be careful. And don't be gone too long."

"We won't," he assured her.

"And Abby," Mrs. Witheridge slipped something secretively into her hand. "You might want to keep this. You'll understand why."

A look passed them between them that Ryan couldn't comprehend. At least, not yet.

"Thank you for helping me last night," Abby whispered to her.

"You're welcome. I charged the bottle in moonlight. Its *batteries* should have enough power to get you through the next couple days."

Abby nodded, but her smile faltered. "I'm not sure it will be enough," she said sadly, and slipped outside without another word.

Chapter 17

❧

"**W**HAT WAS ALL that about back there?" Ryan asked her after they'd put a little distance between themselves and the house.

"Nothing," she said dismissively.

"What did she give you?"

Abby stopped walking and opened her hand. In the middle of her palm sat a shiny, smooth, black stone. "It's an obsidian gemstone. It's meant to protect from harm."

Ryan opened his mouth to tease her about her magical rock, but thought better of it. After last night and his encounter with the wolves, he was at the point where he wouldn't dismiss anything if it could protect them, no matter how silly it seemed on the surface.

"You believe that rock can help?" he asked instead.

"It's not just a rock, it's a gem. They're imbued with special powers from the earth, powers that can be channeled for healing or protection."

"Imbued?"

"It means instilled."

Ah.

"Did she give you an extra one for me by any chance?" he asked.

"Why? Are you feeling oppressed, too?"

"Oppressed?"

"Burdened with worries or troubles."

He flashbacked to the wolves he saw skulking around in the forest. Their teeth.

Abby tilted her head to one side. He knew she was

trying to read him.

"You saw something."

"Maybe," he admitted, shrugging.

"When I was asleep?"

"You mean passed out? Yeah."

They continued walking. He told her about Mrs. Witheridge's witch bottle and having to go outside and dig up soil for her magic. "She's pretty odd," he confided to her in a conspiratorial whisper, even though they were well out of earshot. "She mixed all this weird stuff into a wine bottle and said some magic words. Then she just walked away like she cured you or something."

"She didn't cure me; it was a spell of protection."

Ryan rolled his eyes. "Uh-huh. Well, your 'spell of protection' smelled pretty funky this morning, even with the cork in it."

"I thought it smelled nice."

"You would."

A crow launched itself with a squawk from its

nearby perch and shot across the sky.

"They're a lot alike, Uncle Silas and Mrs. Witheridge," said Abby, watching the bird race across the sky.

"How do you mean?"

"They're *cunning folk*, to use Dad's terminology."

"A medicine woman," Ryan said.

"Exactly."

"Why don't people around here just go to the pharmacy like everyone else?"

"Because pharmacists don't sell cures for illnesses of the heart and mind."

Ryan grinned. "You mean, like, love potions?"

Abby rolled her eyes.

"You think they're somehow connected?" Ryan asked.

"Definitely."

"Do you think Mrs. Witheridge knows more about all this than she's letting on?"

Abby looked down at her shoes. "I don't know,

but that's why we're going to Uncle Silas's place. To look for some answers."

Chapter 18

T HE CABIN WAS just up ahead.

"How many did you see last night?" she wanted to know.

"What?"

"Wolves."

"How did you ...?" Her uncanny ability to read his mind always unsettled him. "Forget it."

He described the wolves to her, and how they seemed to be watching the cottage with keen interest.

"There were maybe three or four," he said. "I

didn't stick around long enough to take a head count."

"Probably the smartest thing you've done in a long time. How big were they?"

Ryan grinned at her sarcasm and shook his head. "*Big*," he said, feeling a cold, clammy sensation on his skin when he recalled their flinty eyes staring at him. "I mean, they were larger than any wolves I've seen in the zoo."

"I see."

They each fell into their own thoughtful silences as they followed the dirt lane back to Uncle Silas's cabin. The sun was climbing through the trees, warming the air. Besides the talkative birds in the woods around them and the scuff of their shoes, the morning was quiet and still.

They approached Uncle Silas's deserted cabin, which looked smaller and even shabbier than yesterday. With all the crisscrossing crime scene tape stitched across the porch, it looked like the set of a horror movie. If a couple of zombies had come staggering out through the door, it wouldn't have surprised Ryan in the least.

They picked their way carefully through the crime-scene tape and climbed the weathered steps, which squealed under their feet like a wounded animal. Then they opened the front door and peered inside.

Well, it was official. They were now criminals, breaking and entering into a house.

An air of sadness and despair hung like a heavy shroud over the place. The gloom was so thick, he could've poked it with his finger and watched it ooze.

There was destruction everywhere. Tables and chairs overturned. Books thrown from bookshelves, lying upside down with their covers sprawled open like dead birds. Pots, pans, silverware, plates and cups tossed helter-skelter, as if a group of gnomes had gone berserk and had a party in their uncle's kitchen. All the glass vials and jars kept in neat, labeled order in the pantry were cast around the room, shattered and emptied. Police lines and markings indicated where evidence had apparently been taken. He knew from watching crime dramas on TV that they were tampering with evidence just by walking around the scene, but he was just as fascinated as Abby by what happened here. Nevertheless, he watched where he stepped as he moved through the living room, although it was hard to avoid crunching glass.

"They were looking for something," Abby murmured as they moved from room to room. She held her hands up in front of her as she walked. Ryan sometimes saw her do that when she was "sensing" a room.

"You mean the police?" he asked.

"No." Abby shook her head. "The ones who come by night."

The foldout bed couch that Abby and Ryan used to sleep on when they were little was torn to pieces, the stuffing hanging out like blooms of yellow algae. "Looks like sharp claws or a knife did that," he said.

"Claws," she confirmed. "Not knives. Do you

smell something?"

Ryan stopped and raised his nose to the air. He recognized at once the sharp, foul stench immediately. The same one on the road leading up to the cabin yesterday.

"What stinks in here?"

Abby said nothing. She stared down the narrow hallway at the other ransacked rooms.

"Abs, what did you mean, 'the ones who come by night'?"

Abby ignored the question and led him down the nearly pitch-black hallway to their uncle's bedroom.

Like the rest of the cabin, the master bedroom was a disaster. Mattress overturned, dresser drawers hanging open, contents spilled to the floor. Papers and clothes strewn everywhere. Only one thing managed to survive the devastation that swept through this room: a painting on the far wall, above the bed. It was a view of the Black Rock river rapids from a high vantage point, winding like a silvery eel through the forested gorge. Uncle Silas painted it a long time ago when he first moved to the mountains. Sometimes he sold his artwork for a little extra cash, but this one he kept for himself. His first painting. And it was pretty good, in Ryan's opinion.

But it wasn't artistic appreciation that drew Abby to the painting now. He could tell she noticed something he didn't. "What is it?" he asked.

"It moved," she said.

"Moved? Everything's been moved in here! Jeez, it looks like Bigfoot had a temper tantrum."

Abby kicked aside some debris so she could get closer to it.

"See?" She pointed to a corner of the frame. Sure enough, Ryan noticed the faded wall color where the frame had shifted.

"So? What does that prove?"

Abby didn't answer. Instead, she reached up, clutched the painting in both hands, and lifted it from the wall. Ryan helped her set it down and lean it against the wall. Then they stepped back in unison and stared at the space on the wall where it had been, hoping to spot something—anything—that might be a clue.

Perhaps a wall safe? A secret compartment of some kind? A map or other clue taped to the wall?

Unfortunately, all they found were a few wispy cobwebs.

"Where *is* it?" Abby said through clenched teeth. "Where did he put it?"

"Put what? What are we looking for, Abs?"

He could tell Abby was trying to dredge up a specific memory of their uncle. "He used to tell me if anything happened to him, he'd leave behind a message. I thought it would be here." Surprisingly, tears glistened in her eyes.

"Look, don't cry. Maybe it's in here." He started riffling through drawers of old junk. He even searched the closet, feeling along the inner wall for anything Uncle Silas might've stuck there.

Nothing.

Abby was on the verge of a meltdown, and he hurried over to console her. "Maybe we should get out of here and get some sunshine. This place is giving me the creeps. I feel like … I don't know … like we're not alone. Do you get that sense, too?"

"I need to find it," she answered him, her voice cracking, "right now!" She stamped her foot hard, and the picture frame, leaning against the wall, fell forward and struck the floor with a loud smack.

They gawked at it.

There, staring up at them, was a code of some sort, scrawled in black marker:

a sphaeth huin nttshae twnoiogdhst

and below it:

6 12 15 15 18 2 15 1 18 4 19

"He must have gone crazy!" Ryan blurted.

"I don't think so," she said quickly, the wheels in her mind spinning. "I think the first part is an anagram, a code where words are formed by rearranging a group of letters. I think I can figure it out. Get me some paper and a pen."

He didn't know where to begin looking, but by some minor miracle, he managed to find a scrap of paper and a broken pencil lying on the floor next to the overturned desk. He hurried back to Abby and prepared himself to be amazed by her ingenuity.

She took the pencil and paper, knelt on the floor, and started re-writing the letters. He waited, breath held tightly, as she played around with the letters, crossing out words and making new ones, looking for a logical pattern.

He sighed. This could take all day. What if the police came back and caught them here? He assumed they were all out looking for their uncle, but for how long? He wanted to tell her to hurry, but he didn't want to risk another meltdown. When Abby was deeply focused on her work, messing with her was like disturbing a nest of snakes.

So instead he watched, occasionally offering a suggestion or pointing out where a letter might make more sense. He knew words too, he reminded her. After all, he was in high school.

But, as Abby pointed out tersely, she knew *puzzles*.

Her fidgety mind worked over the clues of a puzzle like nimble fingers loosening a complicated knot. Never getting frustrated, never complaining, Abby could spend all day hunched over a Sudoku or Kakuro puzzle, or mulling the outcomes of a logic problem. Their mother called her perseverance admirable, but Ryan always thought it kind of odd for a kid her age. It was almost as if she *couldn't* quit, as if stopping anything she started would be an unbearable failure. He didn't think beating yourself up over a puzzle was very admirable. Sometimes you needed to know when you were beat, didn't you?

"These don't make any sense." Abby sighed, frustrated. "These words don't tell me anything. I can't figure it out."

He took the paper and read aloud the words she had written: "House, ghost, night, path, woods, sing, death."

The last one turned his blood cold.

"Maybe you're not looking at it the right way," he told her. "Sometimes we look past the obvious answers when we're overthinking things."

"So, don't think about it so much," she concluded, playing with her hair.

"Right." He wasn't sure if his advice helped Abby or not, but at least she wasn't ripping his head off, so that was a good sign.

Abby sat back and sighed. "If Uncle Silas wrote this in a hurry, which it looks like he did from the scrawled handwriting, he would not have had time to formulate a complex anagram. The solution *must* be simple."

"Probably right before your eyes," he agreed.

Abby studied the original jumble of letters again carefully, no longer writing anything down, just looking for any kind of pattern that made sense.

Then, at last, she jumped to her feet, and a shout of glee escaped her throat.

"Ryan, look!" Frantic, she scribbled letters down in a row that looked like this:

APATHINTHEWOODS

Then she spaced the string of letters into words:

A PATH IN THE WOODS

Together they gasped.

"It's our first clue!" Abby squealed.

Ryan gazed at the paper skeptically. "What do you suppose it means? Was Uncle Silas taken down some path in the woods somewhere? If so, which one?

There must be *thousands* of paths in these woods! How will we know where to find him?"

"Stop being such a dour, dubious, unimaginative doubting Thomas!" she cried, unleashing the full fury of her vocabulary on me. "At least we know one thing: Uncle Silas knew where he was being taken!"

"Did he?" He supposed he *was* being a doubting Thomas, because he didn't see the connection. "Or could the clue mean something else?"

Abby scowled and huffed at him. She didn't like it when he questioned her.

As Ryan stood behind her pondering the meaning of the clue, he was suddenly struck with an insight. All at once things started to make sense to him.

"If Uncle Silas knew where he was being taken, then maybe he also knew who was taking him!"

"Or *what* was taking him," Abby corrected, glancing around the room at the excessive damage caused by some furious force.

Silence fell over them.

"Wait a minute." Abby studied the code again with renewed interest. "I think there's another clue here." She scribbled the rest of the unused letters, spacing the words out like before.

When she was done, all the color drained from her face. Her legs wobbled beneath her as she stood up from the floor.

"Look at this." Shakily, she passed the piece of paper to him.

The remaining letters indeed gave a second clue, this one making Ryan regret his decision to tag along on this vacation.

SHE HUNTS AT NIGHT

"Now what does *that* mean?" His voice had a tremor in it he couldn't iron out. "Who hunts at night?"

"I don't know," she conceded. "Let me work on the second clue."

Abby turned the paper over and copied the list of numbers down. He heard her tell herself, *"Don't overthink, Abby, don't overthink!"* several times, and couldn't help smiling to himself.

"Look at this!" she announced a minute later. On the paper she'd written:

F L O O R B O A R D S
6 12 15 15 18 2 15 1 18 4 19

"Each number represents a letter in the alphabet!" he exclaimed. "How did you figure it out?"

"Uncle Silas and I used to write coded messages like these all the time together when I was little. Don't you remember?"

He shook his head. Maybe he was too busy fishing to notice. As Abby liked to say to him, *You really don't notice anything, do you?*

"Now what do we do?"

Abby started crawling around on her hands and knees, running her fingertips along the edges of the floorboards. "We look for a loose floorboard, obviously." she replied. "There must be something hidden that he wanted us to find."

Made sense.

He dropped to his knees and helped Abby search. They poked and pried at every crevice they could find until their nails started to bleed. Yet all of the boards they tried were nailed tight to the joists underneath. One of them had to be loose, however, or else the message didn't make any sense. Ryan slid over to the closet and started prying at the floorboards there. On the second one, he felt a wiggle.

"Abby, come over here! I think I found something!"

The floorboard was loose, all right. He dug the tips of his nails into the crack and pulled. The board, about twelve inches long, lifted a few millimeters. He kept prying it up until, to his surprise, it popped right out.

"What's down there?" Abby breathed.

"I don't know," he said, hesitating to reach in. He

imagined some grotesque insect or rodent making its nest in that dark cavity under the floor, and he didn't want to get bitten or scratched. However, they'd come too far to be deterred by creepy-crawlies.

Holding his breath, Ryan reached his hand into the darkness and touched something made of rough, grainy wood. A box.

The magic is in the box.

He brought it up into the light and carried it over to the window to inspect it more closely.

The box was made of varnished oak or cedar and weighed at least five pounds. Clearly, it was old, yet well cared for, based on the condition of the oiled hinges. It was about ten inches long and three inches deep. Ryan opened the lid and gawked. Inside lay a worn, leather-bound journal, and next to it a small glass bottle tinted a dark amber. A sluggish liquid filled most of the bottle. A brown cork, sealed by wax, plugged the top.

Without thinking, Ryan was about to pull the cork

out when Abby grabbed his hand.

"What are you doing?" She looked at him like he was crazy.

"I don't know. Checking it out, I guess."

"You don't know what's in it!"

"What are you afraid of? You think Uncle Silas would have led us to a vial of poison?"

"Medicine is poison in large enough doses."

He couldn't argue with her there.

"We don't know what we're dealing with yet," she continued, "that's all."

Abby was right. Who knew what this goopy stuff was inside the bottle?

Besides, the bottle was growing uncomfortably hot in his hand. He set it down on the bed and looked at his palm. It was already beginning to turn red where it'd made contact with his skin.

Witchy things.

Abby stared at the bottle. She also looked like she wanted to touch it but thought better of it.

"Abby ..." Ryan started to say.

"I know. This is what Mom wanted us to find."

Ryan stared at her. How long was she going to keep this little secret from him?

"She told you about the 'magic in the box' too?" he asked.

Abby sat down on the edge of the bed.

"I hear you two talk sometimes. What else has she told you?"

Abby was silent, both hands fidgeting with her hair as she mulled the question.

"Mom just said there might be a way to help cure her, if we talked to Uncle Silas. He has many potions and medicines here. But since he's not here ... I'm guessing this is what she's talking about."

"We need to get this to her fast!"

She rolled her eyes at him. "I don't see that happening quite yet. Let's take a look at the book."

They turned their attention to the journal. It was small and black with a hand-sewn binding, its pages yellowed with age. An old book by the looks of it, possibly centuries old. He fanned through some of the pages, sending dust motes flying into the air.

"It's a journal," he said, amazed.

Abby rushed over and snatched the book from his hands. "Hey, be careful with it," he warned her. "It looks very fragile."

She scanned the first page. "It's the diary of Josiah Martin, dated winter, 1692." She inspected the rest of the book, each subsequent page making her eyeballs pop out even farther from her head until they looked like they were ready to fall from her face. Ryan thought back to something his mother once told him.

"Before Mom was married, wasn't her maiden name Martin?"

If Abby heard his question, she didn't act like it. "This is not only our ancestor's diary but also his *grimoire*, Ryan. He lived in Salem during the witch trials."

"Grimoire?"

"A book where a witch writes down all of his or her spells, and whatever else they want. It's sometimes called a Book of Shadows."

"I guess we found another clue," he said.

"This could explain everything."

"Like what?"

She looked at him like he was a dunce. "Like who we are, and what our role is in all this."

"Or it could leave us even more in the dark."

"You are so obtuse," she complained, wandering over to the window to have a contemplative moment.

Outside, the trees all looked like they were sagging a bit, their branches locked together like mourners at a funeral.

"He's out there somewhere," she whispered. Ryan drew closer so he could hear her. "I wish he were here with us now. I have so many questions. We never finished the training."

"Training?"

Abby took a deep breath. "Uncle Silas was

teaching me about magic, its uses, and what it was all about. He showed me many things—beautiful things—about the world. I learned so much from him that I've never told anybody. But he wasn't finished. He told me, if I'm to belong to the coven one day, I need to complete my training in the dark arts."

"*Coven*? Abby, you're a fifth grader at Carson Elementary School. You live at 15 Overlook Road in Schenectady, New York. You're just a regular kid. Gifted and talented and a little quirky, but still just a kid. Hate to burst your bubble, but it's true. You're no witch."

She gave him a withering look. "Uncle Silas is a warlock, or a male witch. All the stories you've heard about him are true."

"That's impossible!" he shouted. "Real witches aren't real. Besides, if they were, they'd be evil."

"No," she said. "Not all of them; that's a myth. But I'm convinced there is a dark witch in our midst." She pointed out the window.

"On the path in the woods."

"At the *end* of the path," she corrected.

Ryan began pacing the floor. "This is all … I don't know …"

"Haven't you seen enough in the last two days to convince you?"

"There must be a logical explanation …"

"You're trying to explain the irrational with the rational. It doesn't work. Open your mind to the possibility that what we see isn't all there is."

He laughed, but not at her. Not at anything, really. It was just his normal reaction to someone spouting off nonsense and absurdities—the sort that contained hints of uncomfortable truths.

"Okay," he said, throwing his hands up in the air in surrender. "Suppose I believed you."

"Suppose you do."

"What then?"

"Well, then you become enlightened."

Ryan laughed again. "Like a Buddha."

"No." She shook her head. "Like someone willing to take his first step to recognizing his higher power."

"What?"

"If Uncle Silas is a witch, descended from a bloodline of witches, as I believe him to be, then that means Mom has witch blood in her and so do we."

Ryan felt the caress of an icy hand on his skin.

"I-I don't know. I've never ridden on a broomstick before," he said sarcastically.

"Don't be ridiculous. Broomstick riding is folklore. It's Harry Potter stuff. Witches travel like everyone else, but they understand the natural world much, much better."

"Then tell me," he said, determined not to be afraid to hear the rest of the story. "What did Uncle Silas teach you?"

A small, hopeful smile dawned on her face. "You really want to know? Are you sure you won't find it 'quirky' of me?"

"No more than anything else, I guess. I want to

know about magic," he insisted. "*All* of it."

"Then listen without interrupting," she said.

Chapter 19

WHEN ABBY WAS eight years old, her uncle promised to teach her the secret of magic.

They always enjoyed long walks together in the forest, listening to the restless quivering of life. Unlike her brother, who liked to swim, fish, run around with other rowdy boys, and generally make a lot of noise, Abby longed for the solitude of the deep forest.

What Abby enjoyed most, however, was listening to her uncle speak of the treasures contained within nature, of the wonders contained in even the most ordinary objects.

"Do you see this?" He stooped and pointed to the ground.

There, poking up from the dirt, was a white-tipped root.

"It's called Angelica root," he explained. Above his thickening, gray-streaked beard, his blue eyes sparkled. He dug into his pocket and withdrew a pen knife. He sliced the tip of the root off and showed it to her. "I need it for the medicine I'm making."

"It smells like celery."

Uncle Silas smiled. "Indeed it does."

"I thought you made magic," said Abby.

He chuckled softly. "You could say medicine is magic," he replied. "Nature is the greatest magician of all, weaving her power into everything you see around you. From the clouds in the sky, to the birds in the trees, and all the way down to the burrowing insects. All of it exists as one, like a circle. The cloud makes the rain that nourishes the flowers and trees. The trees produce fruit to feed the animals, and the flowers the nectar to feed the insects. Without the animals and the insects, the trees and flowers do not have reason to live. Take away one, and you lose the others. Do you understand?"

Abby nodded. "I think so."

"People are just as connected to the world, my dear. We breathe its air; we drink its water. We depend on the sunshine as the plants and the animals do. We can no more remove ourselves from nature than a goldfish can remove itself from its bowl."

She giggled, imagining her goldfish at home building a tiny ladder to escape from its bowl.

"People have understood this connection for centuries," he went on, "and they've used magic to influence other people and events—sometimes for good, sometimes for evil. Shamans and witch doctors have used the natural ingredients of the forest since ancient times to cure diseases and even cast spells."

"Spells?"

"Magic, my child." He moved over to a tree stump and sat down, inviting Abby to join him. "You see, magic comes from within you. It's a part of your energy that makes you human. We all have magic inside of us, though most people prefer to see themselves as robots—self-reliant, automated machines that exist outside of nature."

She laughed. "That's impossible."

"Yes," he said, "you're right. Humans have will power; we have free choice. We can cast good spells in this world, by our words and our actions, and the earth will thank us for it. Or we can cast evil upon others, and then the world becomes a dark place."

"Do you need a wand?" Abby wanted to know. She didn't quite understand why her uncle belly-laughed so loudly.

"No, I don't need a wand," he finally said, wiping tears away from his eyes. "Magic doesn't work that way. I can't cast lightning bolts out of my hands or dispel demons with a few magic words. Magic glides smoothly, like the waves of an electric current, over everything it touches. Changing it, ever so slightly, until those changes become bigger ones."

"Once my mom was very sick," Abby confided in a whisper. "She was in the hospital for a whole week. It was something to do with her stomach. I prayed every night, wishing as hard as I could that she'd get better. Then, one day, Daddy brought her home. She was healthy again! I think my prayers helped."

Uncle Silas patted her knee and smiled at her. "They did," *he said quietly. "And it was because you believed."*

Abby skipped away happily to look for more of those roots he'd shown her. She was going to be his special helper, she decided, and make him proud.

After a few minutes of poking and prodding the ground, digging up wiggly things and slimy things and things for which she had no name, she was suddenly struck with a serious question.

"But how do you do magic, Uncle? I mean, where exactly does it come from?"

"Let me show you, Abby," he said, beckoning her to his side once more.

Eagerly, she sat down again on the stump next to him.

"It's in here," he said, pointing to her heart. "The source of your power and all your magic. It takes its energy from the air that you breathe, the food that you eat, and the thoughts in your mind. You must first learn how to build your power up, and then release it when you're ready."

He folded his hands together and brought them slowly to his chin. He closed his eyes, and his lips quivered with whispered words. Abby couldn't make most of them out—they sounded like gibberish. He rocked gently for several seconds, like she'd seen old men do in church when they were praying, and then suddenly stopped and stood up. Something told Abby to stand with him, though she wasn't sure why.

Uncle Silas reached down and clasped Abby's hand. He exhaled a deep sigh and grinned at her. The lines on his face smoothed out. A glowing aura of soft white light surrounded his head. She was surprised at how young he looked.

"Do you feel it, Abby?" she heard him ask, though his lips never moved.

"I do," she answered him, without speaking a word.

It was a tingle at first in the tips of her toes. Then a warmth rolled up her body in steady waves. When it reached her head, she felt her ears buzz, her teeth chatter, and the hairs on the nape of her neck stand on end. She thought about the static electricity ball at the science museum her parents took her to last year. When she touched it, the flow of electromagnetic energy made all her hair stand on end. She felt that way now, only the energy had a positive force behind it that she couldn't quite describe. She felt it spread into her stomach, squeeze her heart and lungs, until it seemed like her chest was ready to explode.

Then it happened ... a sudden quick release! An outpouring of energy, glowing a radiant yellow, flowed from her heart and spread over the plants and trees and grasses before her. The plant life shivered when it felt the warm energy, curled and vined and twisted into an archway, forming a tunnel of sorts through the woods. Abby laughed in joy at the spectacle, awed by the power. When she looked up at Uncle Silas, she saw him smile the widest smile she'd ever seen in her life, as though he were feeling true happiness for the first time in his life.

"Go on." He pointed to the path that opened before her. "See what the woods have to show you."

Slowly, she stood and followed the path. She heard the plants shiver delightfully. Heard a chorus of birds sing sweetly overhead, swooping and diving around her. A hummingbird floated in the air mere inches from her face, so close she could feel the air fanning from its wings. "Why, hello there!" she giggled. Then the bird lifted into the air and was gone, replaced by a fluttering cloud of black and orange monarch butterflies welcoming her.

"Uncle Silas, it's so beautiful!" she exclaimed.

Then in a heartbeat it was gone. The trees, the birds, the sky itself ... wiped from existence in the blink of an eye. She stood all alone in complete darkness. A void. Deep and endless and silent. Darkness so thick it felt like it was smothering her. A sharp, foul stench, the breath of the darkness itself, burned her nose. She twirled round and round, trying to find where everything went. But there was nothing to be found. No sign of the light.

A chill bit into her bones.

"Uncle Silas?" she called in a panic. "Where did you go? Where am I?"

A hand dropped suddenly on her shoulder. She screamed. Strong arms grabbed her, and then she heard her uncle say softly in her ear, "It's all right, child. I've got you."

"What is it?" she asked, leaning against his body for safety. "Did I do something wrong?"

"No," he answered calmly above her. "You have done nothing wrong, my child. You have done everything right! You have shown me that you have a good heart and a strong mind."

"Then where did the magic go? Where are we?"

"The magic has not gone; it has merely transformed. This is the heart of evil, the black of night." His voice turned grim. "Empty. Cold. Filled with fear and hatred. Just like a good heart produces bright, joyful magic, a dark heart creates death. The magic is equally powerful, but much more destructive."

Abby groaned. "I'm scared. Why are you showing me this?"

Uncle Silas whispered so close to her ear she could feel his whiskers tickle her skin. "There is something you must know."

"What is it?"

"You need to know the truth about the witch."

She shuddered. "Witch?"

"The one we imprisoned a long, long time ago. The one we can never allow to go free. She is a sorceress of the dark arts who condemned many innocent people to their deaths."

Abby moved deeper into her uncle's embrace. "Is she here? I don't want to see her if she's here."

"She is locked up. The others help me keep her that way. She can never get out."

"What others?"

When no answer came, she asked, "Why are you telling me

this, Uncle?"

"You have a great power, Abby. You will need it one day to continue our mission. Generations before you have helped keep the witch hidden away from mankind. One day your time will come to help as well."

"When?"

"When you are ready."

Chapter 20

RYAN SHOOK HIS head in disbelief.

He had no idea. About any of it. Had he been blind about his uncle and Abby all this time, willfully ignoring what was right before his eyes? It was beginning to make more sense to him now, all the strange experiences he'd had with his sister, and his uncle's unusual ways.

"What happened?" he asked. "I mean, how did you get out of that … dark place you were in?"

"It just blinked out," she answered slowly. "The

same way it appeared in the first place."

"Blinked out?"

"It was magic, Ryan." She looked at me and smiled. Then she glanced at the bottle on the bed and her expression turned earnest. "We have to get back to Mrs. Witheridge's house right away."

"Why?"

"We need to find out everything we can about the witch, where she lives, and how we can stop her."

"You really believe Uncle Silas was kidnapped by a witch?"

"Kidnapped and soon to be killed."

She hunts at night.

"Then that means" —his head was spinning with Abby's story and the revelations it brought— "our only hope is to use magic."

"White magic, yes," she said, taking my hand and leading me to the door. "The good kind, like Uncle Silas practices. And Mrs. Witheridge. We need it to find the witch and stop her."

"Hold on." He let go of her hand and went to the closet. "I want to put this board back. In case what you say is true, we don't want anyone finding our uncle's secret hiding spot."

Abby waited impatiently, tapping her foot.

As he started sliding the board back into place, he heard something. A rattling sound coming from down the hall.

From the front door.

Someone was coming inside!

Abby and Ryan looked at each other in alarm. Should they hide or go see who it was? What if the sheriff had come back to investigate the cabin some more? They would be in big trouble!

As Ryan scanned the room for good hiding spots, Abby bolted from the room. "Wait!" he called to her, but she was gone, scampering down the hallway. He quickly put the book and bottle back in the box and followed. Abby rushed to the front door and opened it without hesitation. There, standing on the porch, was the boy they'd seen in the woods spying on them yesterday.

"What are you doing here?" Abby demanded with unusual hostility.

Stunned by her greeting, the boy's eyes widened, and he stuttered, "I was just l-l-looking for you."

"Well, you found us," she said. "Who are you?"

"I ain't n-never seen you before."

"That's because we don't live around here," Ryan answered, moving past Abby and onto the porch. "We're visiting our Uncle Silas."

"Well, he ain't here."

Ryan couldn't help laughing at the absurdity of the statement. "We noticed."

The boy looked down at his dirty bare feet. "I ain't meanin' to spy, it's just … I need to talk to you about—" He cocked his head inquisitively and stared at Abby. "You got the Sight, don'tcha?"

Abby's eyes narrowed. "Who are you?" she repeated.

"I-I'm Henry Alden." He explained how he lived on the other side of Black Rock Lake with his father. Henry was tall and lanky, about twelve years old, with a gray, unhealthy complexion, and big purple bags under his eyes. It looked as though he hadn't slept very well in the last few nights.

"What's your name?" he asked, holding out a grubby hand.

To his utter amazement, Abby reached out and grasped the boy's hand. He'd never seen Abby shake anyone's hand before. She usually didn't like to be touched in any way by strangers. As he watched, he noticed her grip getting tighter and tighter until Henry's fingers turned white and his face contorted into a grimace of pain.

"Abby..." Ryan said, but before he could break her grip, she dropped Henry's hand and backed up a step. A sheen of perspiration coated her face.

"You're one of us," she said, breathing hard. "Fascinating!"

Chapter 21

※

“WHAT DO YOU mean, 'one of us'?” Ryan asked her. They all sat down on the edge of the porch.

Abby blinked her eyes several times and shook the cobwebs out of her brain. “What?”

“You said 'one of us.'”

Abby twisted her hair. “I did?” She sounded like she just woke up from a dream.

“Never mind.”

He turned his attention to Henry, who watched

their exchange with a mixture of amusement and curiosity.

"So what are you doing here?" Ryan asked.

"I know w-what happened to Mr. Martin," the boy said. "At least, I think I do."

He told a wandering tale about how his mother died in a car accident earlier that year, and how he fought a lot with his dad. This led to him spending most of his time exploring—and possibly living—in the woods, which apparently included keeping a close eye on the comings and goings at their uncle's cabin. Judging by his ripped and grass-stained jeans, Ryan believed him. Even the boy's neck and face were smeared with mud, and patches of his hair were caked with dirt, like he'd been sleeping in the woods for days.

"I ain't a r-runaway, if that's what you're thinkin'," he said to Ryan, as if reading his mind.

"I didn't say—"

"I know what you s-said."

Ryan shot Abby a look. Was it possible Henry had

the same power as she did? To know things and hear things that other people couldn't? Is that what she meant when she said 'one of us'?

Ryan noticed that Henry struggled to stay on topic, so he brought him back to his original statement with a question. "So where is Uncle Silas?"

"Huh?"

"You said you knew."

"Oh, yeah. Sorry. Sometimes I f-forget what I was saying."

He took a moment to gather his thoughts. When he spoke again, the quaver in his voice was gone.

"The witch got him."

Ryan's eyebrow arched skeptically. "What witch?"

"The one who lives in the woods, in the cabin no one can see. 'Cept I can see it. So can the others."

"Others?"

"Mr. Martin, Mrs. Witheridge, and … my ma."

His eyes clouded with sadness.

"Why can they see it but others can't?" Ryan asked.

"They have the Sight." He glanced at Abby. "Like you got."

Abby nodded. "Tell us more about the witch."

"They say she's lived around these parts for years; centuries, even. Her familiars haunt the woods. You let a pet out after sunset, it ain't comin' back."

Ryan and Abby exchanged looks. The signs for lost pets at the General Store. The terror the storekeeper displayed while talking about the woods at night. It made sense now. People around here were afraid of a superstition, or at least that's how Ryan saw it.

"Who is this witch?" Ryan wanted to know. "What's her name? Where exactly does she live?"

Henry stared at him funny. "You don't wanna know, trust me."

"I do," Abby stated.

The quaver returned to his voice. "I-if you go lookin' for her, she'll f-find you first. Then you're dead!"

Henry shot to his feet and started dashing around in circles, flailing his arms and kicking his feet, as if fending off invisible assailants.

"What are you doing?" Ryan said.

Henry stopped and gawped at him. "I don't know. Havin' fun is all. Don'tcha know how to have fun?"

"There isn't anything funny about this," Abby told him. "Where is the witch? If she has Uncle Silas, we need to get him back."

"Blood moon rises tomorrow." Henry gazed up at the sky, squinting. "She comes then."

"What do you mean?"

"That's what my Ma always said. I'd hear her say to my dad, 'Got to do our duty before the blood moon rises.'"

Abby clutched the box containing the book and the vial of potion tightly to her chest. "What duty?"

"She ain't never told me." He covered his mouth with his grimy hands and giggled.

"Why are you laughing?" Ryan demanded.

221

"Because I followed them out to the woods last time, years ago. I seen it with my own eyes what they do out there. I heard the witch's voice and her screams. She hates them all.; she hates all of us!"

"Calm down, Hen—"

"If you go out there, she'll kill you too! Like she killed my mother!"

"You said it was an accident!" Ryan was practically yelling at the kid, but he didn't care.

"Ain't no accidents round here," Henry barked at him.

Henry's gaze dropped to the box in Abby's arms. "You think you got answers in that?"

"That's what I'm going to find out," Abby responded calmly.

"Well, the answers might getcha k-killed."

With that, Henry turned and started skipping away, swinging his arms awkwardly out from his body in an apparent game of some sort. Then he stopped suddenly and looked back, the anger on display a moment ago replaced by a friendly grin.

"You know, if you gotta do this, you d-don't have to do it alone."

"What do you mean?" Ryan asked.

"I'm just s-sayin'. If you need me, I'll help ya out. Remember: I know the way to the witch's cabin."

A path in the woods.

Ryan shrugged. "We don't even know where you live. How will we find you?"

"You ain't gotta know. I'll be around … I always am!"

Chapter 22

AN HOUR LATER they were back in their room at Mrs. Witheridge's house, sitting on Abby's bed, holding the antique box on their laps. Slowly, Abby opened the top and lifted the book out. She handed it to Ryan, who held it like the fragile artifact that it was, and then removed the amber-tinted vial of liquid and set it on the nightstand next to the witch bottle. They stared at the tiny vial, as if waiting for something to happen.

Neither one of them spoke a word, but they each thought the same thing:

I wish we could get out of here now and go save Mom.

Ryan wanted to grab it, stuff it in his pocket, find his dad's keys, and drive home as fast as he could. He didn't have his driver's license yet, but who cares? Their mother was at home suffering, while her sister took care of her. How much more could she take?

But he kept those thoughts to himself. Abby would have probably agreed with him that their mother needed this potion now, but their uncle was still missing, and there was the witch to contend with.

Ryan seethed in silence. *Why did everything have to be so complicated?*

When he looked up, he noticed Abby staring at him. Her little mouth was turned down, her eyes filled with sadness and longing.

"I miss her, too," she murmured, and covered Ryan's hand with her own.

"You need to believe." Her hand squeezed his

fingers tightly.

"What do you mean?"

"You still doubt her existence."

Ryan snorted in derision. "Listen, Henry has a few screws loose. He's different, you know?"

"Why?" She frowned at him. "Because he stutters?"

"No, I don't mean that. I think he spends a little too much time in these woods and has an overactive imagination. I bet he doesn't have any friends."

He winced when he said the last part. Abby turned away and dropped her hand from his.

"I'm sorry, Abs," he said quickly. "It's just ... I mean, do you really believe in this whole witch business?"

"You saw Uncle Silas's cabin."

"Yeah."

"And you saw the raven that flew into your room the other night."

"Yeah."

Abby steepled her fingers and started rubbing her forehead with them. He recognized it as one of her gestures of frustration.

"And you know what she looks like."

"I don't—"

Abby glanced sharply at him. "You saw her. In your dream. She almost drowned you."

The thing with claws for hands and eyes as dead as stones.

He'd almost forgotten about the dream.

Almost.

Now, thanks to Abby, the details came flooding back to him, the horror fresh and new all over again.

Ryan's eyes slid over to the witch bottle next to the bed. "Well, let's suppose there's something going on around her. What about that thing? Isn't that supposed to protect us?"

"One witch bottle isn't strong enough. Actually, I don't think a hundred would be either. Besides, without *this,* nothing is going to stop the witch." She pointed to the small vial of liquid.

227

"But I thought that was some sort of cure for Mom?"

"It is," she responded, "or at least, I hope it is. But magic cuts both ways. It could probably cure … or kill."

"We should give it to Mrs. Witheridge right away. She might know what to do with it."

"Yes," Abby agreed, "but not yet."

"Why not?"

"Because first I want to read this." She took the book from his lap. The old leather binding creaked as she opened it. She squinted at the tiny, scrawled wisps of faded writing on the page. "The ink has faded so much that it's hard to read."

"Give it to me."

Ryan laid down on the bed next to the window, so he could capture as much of the fading light as possible and started to read to Abby.

"The first entry is dated January 30, 1692."

"Near the beginning of the witch mania," Abby

informed him, as she settled back on the bed next to
him to listen.

FROM THE JOURNAL OF
JOSIAH MARTIN
JANUARY 30, 1692

*Salem village bears witness to the darkest of circumstances,
in this, the Year of our Lord, 1692. It afflicts the hearts and
minds of His pure and righteous people. A malevolency of spirit
descends upon us all and has begun to turn neighbor against
neighbor.*

*The fierce grip of winter and a smallpox epidemic ravages
our community. My wife Sarah has become stricken with the
disease. She is bedridden and suffers greatly.*

I pray for her recovery, but each day my heart grows heavier and heavier with despair. I would do anything to bring her back to full and vibrant health.

FEBRUARY 2, 1692

The Indian wars have nearly reached our borders, only seventy miles away from Salem, and refugees flood our village daily from the ransacked towns of New Hampshire and Maine. The heathens have burned and destroyed their homes. Theirs is a desperate lot, whom the Lord no doubt led to our humble community, for we, as His servants, would give charity to any pious Christians who call upon us.

Yet the strain on our community is great. Dark days as these breed conspiratorial thoughts. The Reverend Parris sermonizes constantly on the need for vigilance against the Arch Enemy.

Even the children in Meeting have begun to act strangely. Poor Betty Parris, the Reverend's little daughter, and her cousin Abigail Williams, delight in laughter and odd games during the most solemn of homilies. They claim bewitching influences for their disconcerting behavior in Meeting.

Curse of the Witch

Whispers of the girls' behavior and motives have reached all corners of the village. I fear the gathering of dark clouds on the horizon.

FEBRUARY 5, 1692

My poor Sarah suffers greatly still from the smallpox. She is feverish and hallucinates nightly. Her skin is sallow and her face as gaunt as one who is ready for the grave. My heart aches. Death waits eagerly to harvest her soul, but I cannot bear to let her go.

The men and women who enter my mercantile all speak on the matter of death, and nary are they charitable. "The Devil be amongst us," and, "Witches curse our village," are the common sentiments. I ask whither such grim talk ascends, and they relate to me the story of Tituba, the Reverend Parris's Indian slave girl, and her bewitching of the girls Betty Parris, Abigail Williams, and young Ann Putnam.

I ask how this could be—what manner of witchcraft doth she practice? They tell me of the parlor games she plays with the girls in the Parsonage: the fortune telling, and the Venus glass.

Portends of the future are her specialty.

All go unnoticed in the Reverend's own house? I ask.

Aye, they tell me in earnest, for Tituba's bewitching spells make fools of even the most virtuous of men!

I am conflicted. The Bible claims we shall not suffer a witch to live, yet if the stories of Tituba's extraordinary and far-reaching powers are true, how can I resist the temptation to call on her? What prophecy might she have on my poor Sarah? What magical elixir might she concoct that could save her life?

FEBRUARY 7, 1692

I visited Tituba this evening, after sending word through her husband, John Indian, who frequents my shop often for supplies, that I wished to make enquiries into her magic. He agreed, in his usual amiable way, to have me meet her, though his countenance suggested the utmost caution. I agreed such caution was prudent. Talk of witchcraft amongst the village was spreading, and old quarrels over property and possessions were heating up. The winter and the smallpox epidemic were straining people's charity.

Curse of the Witch

I waited in the trees behind the Parsonage for the last candle to go black before approaching. John Indian met me at the back door. He beseeched me to whisper and tread lightly, so as not to awaken the girls or Reverend Parris.

Tituba met me in the small room in the back of the Parsonage, which served as hers and John Indian's quarters. She is a bold and striking figure. Hard lines of experience etch her face. Her eyes, dark and deep-set, glitter with knowledge of forces for which I have no account. And though her stature is slight, she carries herself with strength and unfaltering dignity.

We sat across from each other at a small table as I explained the meaning of my calling. Tituba looked upon me with sympathy, for she knew my Sarah, and thought highly of her. "Tituba not see everything," she warned me in her coarse West Indies' accent. "Tituba sees what is revealed to her." I told her I understood that she would do her best.

Tituba grasped both my hands and turned them palms up so she could scrutinize them avidly. She uttered noises under her breath, words I did not understand, and then closed her eyes. She swayed and groaned, as if communing with unseen forces, and when she opened her eyes again, she smiled.

"Fear no more, Mr. Martin. Tituba sees a cloud shaped like a dove, and sun where there was only darkness."

My heart rejoiced! I took her meaning in the most constructive of ways, paid her handsomely for her services, and left the Parsonage a man relieved of his burdens.

FEBRUARY 9, 1692

The sun has broken through the winter gloom and I saw the sky, bright and blue as a jewel, for the first time in weeks. And I saw, much to my heart's delight, a cloud shaped like a morning dove, hovering on the horizon!

Without hesitation, I went to check on Sarah. Several of our servants were gathered around her, muttering proclamations of a miracle. They parted to let me through, and I beheld the sight of my Sarah, her cheeks rosy with color again. She sat up in bed and wept joyfully as I embraced her.

My prayers had been answered! But by whom I would need to ponder.

Curse of the Witch

MARCH 15, 1692

Food is growing scarce in Salem village as the winter drags on, and the dreadful accounts of colonial losses in King William's war with the Indians has made many people frightened of unseen devils.

Abigail Williams, Betty Parris, and Ann Putnam Jr. claim affliction by witches and cry out against many good Puritan citizens of Salem. They cried out first against poor Tituba, who is rumored to have been beaten to confession by her master, Reverend Parris. They cry out as well against Sarah Osborne and Sarah Goode. My Sarah, fortunately, has made full recovery from the plague, and being of saintly disposition, should remain above these ludicrous charges.

Many other men of education and means agree with me about witchcraft. We believe such nonsense as "spectral evidence" should be inadmissible in court. Yet magistrates Hathorne and Corwin accept, unquestioningly, the rants and raves of these fanatical girls.

The accused are provided no counsel before being brought before the court, where they are questioned mercilessly, and their bodies stripped and searched in full public view for the mark of the Evil One. The slightest blemish on the skin is surmised by our half-witted magistrates to be evidence of a witch's pact with Satan.

My heart aches as I watch Tituba and the other women brought before the court, accused and charged with witchcraft, and taken away again to be put in the stocks or thrown in the local jail.

Next, they cry out against Rebecca Nurse, the matriarch of our village. She is seventy years old, and as pious and pure of heart as Cotton Mather himself! I grow angry at the spectacle of witchcraft and the damage it is doing to our way of life. I barely recognize my own village anymore.

JUNE 10, 1692

With a festive air, the hanging of Bridget Bishop takes place on Gallows Hill. I fear the hanging tree will be oft-used this summer, as the witch hysteria shows no sign of abating.

I do not know why I came to witness this spectacle. Perhaps a part of me denies the evidence of my own eyes that our village,

Curse of the Witch

once a place of decency, has rotted from the inside with such vehemence. Perhaps I wait and hope that men of education and status will unite in one voice and demand an end to this deadly farce and the immediate release of all the prisoners. Seldom do such men speak out in calamitous times, however. They find their courage more readily in their homes than in the public square.

So, we watch mutely and guiltily as Sheriff Corwin hauls Bridgit Bishop up the steps to the hangman's rope. There, he slips her head into the noose, and, without a prayer from the solemn and hypocritical Reverend Parris, drops her without a second thought, whereupon her neck breaks as a dry twig snaps in a frost. The creak of the rope will haunt my dreams forevermore, as poignant a thing as the guilt that wracks my soul.

The crowd stares in shock at the sight of Bridgit Bishop's body swaying in the wind. Several women turn their heads from the grisly spectacle and weep into their husbands' chests ... but are their tears of shame or remorse?

What Puritan guilt—if any—fills their hearts?

JUNE 10, 1692

David R. Smith

The thirst for blood in our village appears unquenchable. The trials continue unrelentingly, and today six more people swing for the crime of nothing more than defending themselves in God's eyes. Grief tears me apart.

NOVEMBER 21, 1692

The *Crimes against Sensibility*, as I have come to think of the witch hysteria in Salem, are nearing an end. Magistrates Hathorne and Sheriff Corwin have become sensible to the notion that the afflicted girls cry out against the innocent, and grave mistakes have been made.

Hundreds who had been housed in local jails and imprisoned in Boston are released. I know not the fate of Tituba, for she has not been seen amongst the congregation at Meeting or about the Parsonage. My enquiries go unsatisfied until one day Goody Witheridge, a widower, and George Alden, a fellow member of the gentry who sympathizes with the accused as I do, enter my mercantile and ask if they might sup with me this night. Surprised, I agree to their offer, and we meet at the Alden estate at 6 o'clock where we eat fine meats and drink good wine.

Curse of the Witch

During the feast, they confide in me Tituba's whereabouts. She and John Indian are gone, sold away to a slaver from a new southern settlement, but not before both were beaten cruelly by Reverend Parris. My friends know not the reason for the beatings, but assume they were for transgressions relating to the witch trials.

I express my dismai. I was hoping to rekindle my acquaintance with Tituba. Then Goody Witheridge and George Alden tell me the most amazing tale.

They had been secretly meeting with Tituba last winter prior to the witchcraft outbreak. She had used her Venus glass and the broken egg to portend their futures, and, being pleased with what they'd seen, continued visiting Tituba in secret to learn more of her powers. She taught them about the magic she'd learned in Barbados, the power that surrounds and emanates all living things, and how she learned to see into it and gain insight to the future. She taught them how to mix potions to cure illnesses or heal wounds, and gave them a particularly powerful tincture, one she described as having both the power of life and death in one bottle, depending on the intention of the user. Finally, she shared *her private thoughts on the nature of good and evil, and how the flawed and oppressive Puritan worldview was clouding the minds of the young.*

All my innermost feelings, all my doubts and skepticism, which I would never dare to share with anyone other than my dear wife, were expressed in the words of Alden and Goody Witheridge. The wisdom of God does not reside solely in the words of the Bible or the sermons of the Preacher. And, Tituba claimed, we are not all doomed to the Eternal Flames simply for our flawed human natures. If only Reverend Parris saw fit to share this wisdom at Meeting. It might have healed a lot of broken hearts and souls.

DECEMBER 5, 1692

I had a dream this evening that young Abigail Williams had visited my bed chamber whilst I slept. Her eyes, aflame with cruelty, glowed blood-red in the dark. She cursed me and swore she wasn't through with her crimes, revealing that she was going to the Massachusetts Bay Colony and beyond to cry out against more innocents. This and only this, she swore, would sate the bloodlust of her master.

Curse of the Witch

The next morning Salem Village was astir with rumor. It was reported Abigail Williams had run away from the Parsonage. A mob quickly formed and scoured the village and countryside, but nobody could find the young wench.

The hunt was called off three days later. Reverend Parris, speaking from his pulpit at Meeting, appeared heartbroken as he begged the congregation for their prayers in finding young Abigail. I speak only for myself when I say I am glad we are rid of her. Even Betty Parris and young Ann Putnam seemed relieved to have her gone. The covenant between them was now broken for good, and order was being restored to Salem. Neighbor reconciled with neighbor, and old quarrels were put aside for new friendships. We are truly parting ways with the horror that bled us so deeply.

However, a nagging guilt won't leave me alone. Abigail is out there somewhere, and her evil will only mature as she grows older. Bound by sacrament to Satan himself, Abigail Williams will take her lies and treachery to another innocent community, and the violence will happen all over again.

That is, unless we stop her.

David R. Smith

DECEMBER 6, 1692

We left first thing in the morning. I bade my wife farewell, explaining to her the necessity of our harrowing journey. Sarah agreed it was a just and noble cause, for good men could not abide a witch to be loose among the colonies, especially in such precarious times. I am lucky to have such a wife.

JUNE 19, 1693

We tracked the girl across Massachusetts Bay Colony, and up into Connecticut and New Hampshire. We followed her trail through Maine and Rhode Island, until finally tracking back to New York. In the remote and mountainous hinterlands we discovered a small cabin, whereupon we made a horrifying discovery.

A man and woman, along with their two young children, had been brutally murdered, their bodies almost completely drained of blood. We found them hastily buried in shallow graves, too shallow to keep the animals out. We knew Abigail Williams was hiding inside the cabin. My flesh crawled with the sensation of eyes watching me.

We set about at once with our plan to ensnare the witch with our magic. The witch's familiars were wolves and ravens, and several times we had to fend off attacks whilst we recited our incantations. Thrice the witch appeared, fiendish and bedraggled, less a young woman and more a wild beast, and took to using her black magic to bedevil us. She could make fire appear from her fingertips. She conjured demons who lurked and taunted us from the shadows. When we accosted her, she grunted like a pig, screaming and threatening to unleash her master's full wrath upon us. When we attempted to restrain her, she would twist in our arms like an eel, displacing her own bones with sickening pleasure. Her laughter became harsh and grating, her vocabulary that of a lecherous whore.

We ccould not kill the witch. A new plan was needed. We sought help from the local natives who made their simple homes out of mud and sticks, and knew the land and its magical properties better than anyone. They too sensed the presence of the witch in their midst like a stink wafting off a bog. They feared going anywhere near the cabin, but they were willing to aide our endeavors with the necessary ingredients from the woods.

With their help, and the potent tincture Tituba gave us, we created a powerful spell that trapped Abigail Williams within the cabin. One step over the barrier, and her flesh would burn and putrefy. We watched her attempt to cross the boundary once, cackling the whole time, but then withdraw her leg after it burst into flame. She swatted at the flames with the folds of her cassock and screamed in rage.

We were warned by the Indians that the spell would not last forever. We must renew it on the nights when the Creator Spirit stains the moon with blood. That would be our sign that the magic was waning, and the witch's evil was growing again.

Regrettably, it is a burden all three of us must place on our descendants for all time, for it is only in a coven of three that we have the power to renew the spell. I can never return to Salem village; the risk would be too great. Nor can I ever see my Sarah again, for I would not dare to bring her to this vile and godforsaken place.

Sadly, this remote wilderness will forever be our home.

And our curse.

Chapter 23

RYAN CLOSED THE book and set it on the bed next to him. He looked at it warily like it might spring open on its own, spilling more secrets about their family. The story was incredible.

The rest of the journal's pages were filled with jotted thoughts and scribbled lists: spells, concoctions, and odd astronomical details about the moon, sun, and planets. He supposed it made sense to Abby, but to him it just looked like the ravings of a lunatic. There was nothing more in the book about

Abigail Williams. It was as though Josiah Martin couldn't bring himself to write of the tragedy of his life and the horrors of the witch anymore.

Ryan felt a creeping numbness spread over his body. His emotions were a mixture of sadness and wonder. What must it be like to spend the rest of your life guarding a witch and keeping her from escaping? He could see what Josiah meant by a *curse*. Never going home to Salem again, having to make a new home in a strange and bewildering land.

One question above all, though, occupied his thoughts: Why was Abigail Williams causing all this trouble now? What was wrong with the spell of defense? Why was it faltering?

When he asked her, Abby confirmed his biggest fear: Tomorrow night was a lunar eclipse, and not just any ordinary, run-of-the-mill eclipse: a super blood moon eclipse.

And it was on the night of a blood moon eclipse that the spell of entrapment was cast!

Yet why did it seem like Abigail Williams was growing stronger and more powerful?

Abby read the train of thought going through his mind and answered, "She feels emboldened because the coven is broken."

"What do you mean?" he asked.

"Henry Alden. Recognize the last name? His mother must've been a descendant of George Alden, one of the three who helped Josiah Martin track down Abigail Williams."

"And Mary Witheridge ..."

"Was an ancestor of Mrs. Witheridge." Abby nodded, satisfied her brother was finally putting together the pieces. "It takes three to reinforce the spell and keep the witch trapped in her cabin. If even one of them doesn't show up tomorrow night during the eclipse ..."

Ryan gasped. "The spell is broken!"

"And the witch escapes."

He sat down heavily on the cot. "What are we

247

going to do? Henry's mother is dead…"

"And Abigail Williams has Uncle Silas, leaving only Mrs. Witheridge … and us."

Ryan stared at her. "What do you mean, *us?*"

"We can be the new coven; don't you see? We could cast the spell again and renew the magic. I know I can do it. And Mrs. Witheridge has the power … I experienced that last night. That just leaves … you."

Me.

Ryan burst out laughing. He didn't mean to, but he couldn't help it. He'd only just discovered a little while ago that he had witch blood in him, and now he was expected to battle one of the most notorious villains in American history? One who could control murderous wolves and other creatures and infiltrate his dreams whenever she desired?

"W-what are we going to do?" he asked.

Abby gave him a curious look. "What do you mean? We're going to do what we have to do. Rescue Uncle Silas. Save Mom. And make sure Abigail

Williams never, ever gets out."

"That's a tall order, Abs."

Ryan stood and wandered to the window. It was after seven o'clock and the daylight was already starting to drain from the sky.

"It'll be one heck of a fight."

"I know," Abby agreed. "Abigail Williams may be physically trapped in her cabin, but her influence is growing stronger by the second."

That's putting it mildly, Ryan thought. She had reached into his dreams with feverish intensity, and she almost took Abby's life last night.

And then there was Uncle Silas. Somehow, she had been able to abduct him physically and was no doubt keeping him captive at her cabin. They had to rescue him before the blood moon rose tomorrow night, before the eclipse's shadow was permanently cast over all of them.

As Ryan turned away from the window, a lone howl came from the woods.

He turned back and caught furtive movement coming from the woods directly across from him. A tree branch swayed where something had been hiding.

Ryan scanned the trees, a lump rising in his throat.

There. Over by a thick clump of bushes. A pair of eyes watching him—keenly.

The wolf slinked out of the shadows and stood brazenly watching the house. Watching *him*.

"Abby, come here." He waved her over to him, keeping his eyes locked on the wolf.

She crawled across the bed and kneeled at the window.

Her breath caught in her throat. Behind the first wolf crept several others, fanning out, all facing the cottage with aggressive postures and teeth bared.

"Don't move," Ryan murmured.

The first wolf stepped forward. It held its head low, its flinty eyes narrowed and zeroed in on Ryan. A silvery string of saliva fell from its fangs. A deep snarl rattled in its throat.

"I'll get Mrs. Witheridge," Abby said, leaving the window and crossing to the door.

"Abby, no!"

The wolf sensed their distress and lunged forward. It raced toward the house and stopped just short of the window. Only an inch of glass and windowsill protected Ryan from the crazed animal on the other side.

Ryan felt mesmerized by its eyes. He couldn't look away. A strange, twitching sensation spread through his arms. He felt the muscles spasm and his hands lift toward the glass. His fingers opened on their own and gripped the bottom of the windowsill. A compulsion to open it came over him, a *need* he couldn't resist. He had to let it in. It pounded through his head like a mantra.

Let it in.

Let it in.

"Ryan, what are you doing?" he heard Abby scream at him from far away.

LET IT IN!

But before he could obey the command and seal their doom, Abby jumped on his back and tackled him like a linebacker, sending him sprawling across the bed. The wolf, startled by the commotion, snarled and growled and scratched at the glass furiously before finally retreating with its pack into the woods.

Ryan sucked in a deep breath of air when the spell released him. Whatever invaded his body left just as quickly as it had come. He felt physically and emotionally exhausted.

It was her. Abigail Williams. She knew where they were and would stop at nothing to get to them.

"We need to do something," his sister said, rolling off her brother. "We can't let her keep getting into our heads like this."

Abby got her suitcase out from underneath the bed. Ryan watched in fascination as she withdrew a few items from a zippered pouch beneath her clothes. Two pieces of ordinary looking white rope, a candle, and a book of matches. And a knife that Ryan recognized immediately from his old Boy Scout camping days.

"How did you—?"

She silenced him with a hard look that warned him not to ask any more questions.

"Okay." He put his hands up in submission. He was out of ideas anyway. Maybe more magic was the answer.

Abby placed the candle in the center of the room and sat before it cross-legged. She invited Ryan to join her. Once he was seated across from her, she lit the candle, shook out the match, and closed her eyes. Ryan closed his eyes too, though he had no idea what he was supposed to be thinking about or doing right now. That's okay. Experience taught him it was best just to go along for the ride.

When he opened his eyes, Abby already had the knife in her hand and one of the pieces of the rope. The rope was about twelve inches long. She placed the knife in the middle of the loop she had made in the rope and began to saw it back and forth. As she cut the rope in half, she muttered these words:

> "From you to me this spell I break,
> It was not right for you to make,
> Its path I will abruptly end,
> And back to you this spell I send."

Ryan flinched when Abby cut the cord. He didn't know what to expect. A flash of magic, a little puff of fairy dust perhaps. After all he'd seen, anything was possible. But when nothing immediately happened, he felt disappointed. Had the trick failed?

"It wasn't a *trick*," Abby said irritably.

Abby took the string, now in two pieces, and gazed at the ends she had cut as if expecting a voice to tell her what to do.

"How do you feel?" Ryan asked her. "Do you

think your spell made any difference?"

Abby took a deep breath.

"I feel ... lighter." she said, stretching her arms out and then patting her stomach and legs.

"You don't look any different."

"It doesn't work like that."

"What exactly did you just do?"

"Removed the witch's spell from me. I cut our ties. She hopefully won't be able to read my thoughts anymore and get into my head."

"Maybe I should do it, too," he suggested. "She seems to like to hang out in my mind quite a bit. I was thinking of charging her rent."

"Why do you think I have a second piece of rope?"

As she handed the rope and knife over to Ryan, they heard footsteps coming down the hall. The door opened and Mrs. Witheridge stuck her head inside. "I'm making dinner...." she said, stopping short when she saw the rope and knife in Ryan's hands. Her eyes darted from Ryan, to the candle burning on the floor, and then to Abby. A long look passed between them. Then she said, "Be ready in five minutes," and closed the door.

"You think she knows what we're doing?" Ryan asked when she left.

"I think she knows everything," Abby responded.

Chapter 24

IN THE WOODED countryside, twilight came early.

Thick shadows spilled from the evening sky, cold and blue. They dripped on Abby's skin and made her shiver.

"Move closer to the fire," advised Mrs. Witheridge when she saw the girl shiver.

"I'm all right," she replied, but scooted her chair up closer anyways.

They had spent the better part of an hour toasting

marshmallows and making small talk. Then Ryan announced he was going off to find a fishing pole in Mrs. Witheridge's shed. Abby knew better; it wasn't fishing on his mind. He was looking for a weapon he could wield should the wolves come back tonight.

Abby took a deep breath, sighed, and said, "The moon is beautiful. It'll be full soon."

"Yes, tomorrow night. The blood moon … a total lunar eclipse of the second full moon of the month. Very rare… and very powerful."

For the first time since she could remember, Abby didn't feel like talking about magic.

"I wonder when Dad will be back," Abby murmured, looking around at the darkening wood.

"I don't know."

"Has he called?"

Mrs. Witheridge smiled into the cup of tea she was holding. "Did you forget, dear? I don't have a phone. I prefer solitude."

"I understand," Abby said. "I like being alone,

too."

Mrs. Witheridge nodded slowly. "We're a lot alike, you and I."

When Abby didn't answer, Mrs. Witheridge pressed on: "Is there something on your mind, dear? Something you want to tell me about?"

Firelight glinted in the old woman's eyes.

Mrs. Witheridge was far more perceptive than the average person, which made it harder for Abby to conceal her true thoughts and feelings. In that respect, she was just like Uncle Silas.

"The spell you were casting in your room," Mrs. Witheridge began. "Do you think it will work?"

Abby shifted uncomfortably in her chair. "I … I don't know. I feel better, I guess."

"Better? Like the witch's connection to you has been broken?"

Abby flashed her a look of surprise and terror.

Mrs. Witheridge leaned toward her and said in a hushed tone, "We don't need to pretend anymore that we don't know each other's natures. I've been friends with your uncle for a very long time now. We're partners, of a sort. Bound by a promise made a long time ago."

"A covenant."

Mrs. Witheridge beamed in delight. "You're a fast learner. Yes, a covenant. A sacred blood pact between our ancestors—mine, yours, and the Aldens."

"I met Henry today," Abby confessed, "when we visited Uncle Silas's cabin."

"You were there today?" Mrs. Witheridge's eyes grew in alarm. "You didn't tell me you were going."

"You wouldn't have let us go. I know that."

The old woman smiled slyly. "You're right, of course, I wouldn't have. It's not safe for you two to be walking around that far into these woods. Even in the daytime."

"He told us about a path that leads to the witch's cabin."

Mrs. Witheridge waited, the fire's flames

consuming the whites of her eyes and turning them red as embers.

"I know all about Abigail Williams," Abby continued in a conspiratorial whisper, watching for signs of Ryan's return.

"You do?"

"I read about what happened in Salem and how Josiah Martin and the others struck out to find Abigail Williams. It was in the book."

"What book would that be?"

"Josiah Martin's grimoire. Ryan and I found it under a floorboard in Uncle Silas's closet."

Mrs. Witheridge nodded slowly and threw another log onto the fire, watching it sputter as she poked and rearranged the wood. When she was satisfied with the health of the fire, she set the poker aside and resumed her close appraisal of Abby.

"Did you find anything else?"

Abby looked away.

"Come on, child. I need to know. Tomorrow night

I must perform the Sacrament of Rites to renew the seal that imprisons the witch inside her cabin. If you are holding back from me—"

"We have the potion. The one Tituba gave to Josiah Martin."

Mrs. Witheridge drew her shawl tightly around her shoulders. "Silas always protected it well. I never knew where he kept it, but I always knew it was safe. We used it almost five years ago at the last blood moon. We will need it again tomorrow night."

"It's a small bottle," Abby said, mostly to herself.

Mrs. Witheridge nodded. "Aye, that it is. It won't last forever, and none of us witches alive today knows exactly how Tituba created the formula."

"You mean the magic—?"

"Won't last forever," she finished with a deep sigh. "Hopefully, neither will Abigail Williams."

Abby stared at her.

"You know much more than you let on," observed Mrs. Witheridge. "You see it, don't you, in your mind's eye? You have the most inquisitive, searching, and *perceptive* eyes I've ever seen in one so young. The power glows in you like a lantern."

Abby opened her mouth to say something but closed it again.

"Abigail Williams perceives it, too. She's drawn to you like a moth to a flame, only she doesn't want to bask in your warm glow … she wants to destroy you and take your power for herself."

Abby shivered. "What do you mean?"

"You say you know about Abigail Williams because you read about her in a book. The book tells truths, indeed, but you cannot know a witch like her through mere words on a page."

"What do you mean?" Abby repeated, her voice rising an octave.

"Give me your hand."

Abby hesitated, her heart spiking with fear.

"Give it to me," Mrs. Witheridge insisted.

"Why?"

263

"You must know what you're up against."

She won't let anything happen to me. She needs me—and Ryan—as much as we need her.

"That's right," Mrs. Witheridge affirmed, hearing the girl's thoughts as clearly as music from a summer bandstand. "I need you both. And I need *you* especially to understand."

Abby took a deep breath and slipped her hand into the old woman's. She steeled herself for whatever onslaught of psychic impressions her mind would receive.

She wouldn't have long to wait.

Upon contact with her skin, a crawling sensation, like a swarm of ants, marched up Abby's arm and into her shoulder, followed by a burst of color. Then a reel of images exploded in her mind.

"We are one and the same. Two souls … one blood."

Mrs. Witheridge's words slid through her mind like a cool breeze and were gone just as quickly. Then an image bloomed before her eyes. She saw Mrs.

Witheridge standing by a grave, only she was a much younger woman in the prime of her life, elegantly dressed in a long black evening gown. Standing beside her was Uncle Silas before she ever knew him, a younger man in his thirties, with thick brown hair tied back in a ponytail. Between them stood a white gravestone, the words on its lichen-covered surface almost scrubbed away by time. Abby found herself pulled forward by an inexplicable force. She stood now between her uncle and Mrs. Witheridge, staring down at the grave marker.

ABIGAIL WILLIAMS
1676-

The witch who shares my name, Abby thought.

Then the vision blurred, and with disorienting speed, she was rushed to the edge of a clearing, in the middle of which sat a small cabin. The logs looked freshly hewn, the roof thatched with thick bundles of mud, hay and sticks. A cabin from one of the earliest colonial periods, Abby presumed. Candles lit the interior of the cabin with a dull orange glow. Smoke rose lazily from the chimney.

Then, a figure moved behind one of the windows. Abby watched as a woman in a white bonnet pulled a curtain aside and peered out into the night. She looked worried, afraid, glancing furtively about before drawing the curtain back in place. Abby felt a kinship to the girl, who looked no older than eighteen, but she couldn't explain why.

Why am I here? She looked around for Mrs. Witheridge but was startled to find no sign of her or her uncle. What was she doing out here by herself? Why had she been abandoned? Maybe she was meant to talk to the person in the cabin, but she was afraid. The urge to flee gripped her legs, for even on such a peaceful night, the cabin emanated an aura of evil. She turned to leave when a voice screeched …

"Get out of here, witch!"

Abby jumped and spun around. Somehow the girl in the window had snuck up on her without Abby even noticing and stood before her, screaming hysterically in her face. The girl's innocent, waif-like appearance was gone. *A show for me,* Abby realized. *She hasn't looked like that in over three hundred years.*

The witch's scarlet eyes burned in the sunken hollows of her skull. Shards of teeth poked out of her rotted gums like razors. She screamed again like a tortured animal, her jaw contorting, the bones and ligaments snapping and creaking. A long green tongue stretched out of her mouth and tasted the air like a snake's.

"Did you come here to die like the others, witch?" The voice was hoarse and raspy.

Abby cried out in horror and pushed the foul creature away. The girl, the *thing,* fell to the ground, cursing, and gave chase as Abby fled into the woods.

"Help me, Mrs. Witheridge, help me!"

She heard the thing running behind her like a wild

dog, panting, growling. One moment it was on the ground nipping at her heels; next, it was crashing through the trees overhead. Heavy wings slashed the air. The shrieking caws of a hundred ravens pounded in her ears. Abby's neck bristled as she sensed the witch preparing to lunge at her and sink her teeth into her flesh.

Abby tripped on a root and struck the ground so hard it knocked the wind out of her. She curled up instinctively into a ball, hiding her face from the demonic thing hovering over her. The witch snickered, the sound like dried leaves skittering on pavement.

Abby peeked, her curiosity too strong to resist, and watched the witch take two short lengths of white rope out of a pocket of her tattered cassock. She cackled wretchedly as she showed the strands of rope to Abby, who recognized them at once. The ones she had cut earlier with Ryan. The witch saw the recognition dawn on Abby's face and howled with glee. Wordlessly, she brought the two ends of the ropes together. When they merged, a fiery red glow seared the ends of the ropes together. Little tendrils of smoke snaked into the air.

Abby gasped. The rope was whole again. And just like that, the weight was back on her chest and in her bones again.

Abigail Williams bent over until her face was so close to Abby's that her foul breath stung her nose.

"You can never tear us apart, witch. We are one and the same, and I shall have you as I have your uncle! If you want him back alive, come and get him!"

Abby screamed ….

…and the vison shattered like glass. The witch was gone; the clearing, the woods and the little lonely cabin were gone as well.

Abby found herself sitting once again in the lawn chair in Mrs. Witheridge's backyard; the old woman, now on her knees at Abby's side, soothed the girl in hushed tones. "You're all right, child," she repeated the words until they began to sink in. "You're safe. The witch can't harm you now."

Abby tried to catch her breath. It was several minutes before the horror fully subsided and she could speak again. "Why did you show me that ... that ghastly vision?"

"You must be prepared for what is coming. You are powerful, child ... but Abigail Williams has all the power of Hell at her disposal."

Interlude 3
What he finds in the dark

Pain. It's all he feels. All his joints have stiffened on him, his muscles are cramped and tight, and a deep thirst aches in his throat. He needs to get out, he realizes, but he knows of no escape from this basement. Still, he must try. He must explore his surroundings. Time has almost run out.

Silas Martin tries to stand. At first his legs quiver and tense beneath him and he is not sure if they'll support his weight. He reaches out to steady himself, grabbing hold of a *slimy root that juts out of the earthen wall. He smiles, proud of his little success, of the strength he is surprised to find he possesses. Yet there is no time to waste. He gets moving immediately, feeling around the walls of his prison cell, searching for any means of escape. He needs to hurry before the witch returns.*

His eyes have adjusted to the dark now, at least as well as they ever will, and what he finds in the corner of the basement surprises him. Bones, of various sizes and shapes, are tossed in a heap with careless abandon. He drags his eyes across the rest of the cellar and finds more bones littering the floor. Curiosity compels him to pick one of them up. At once, images swarm his mind, and he bears witness to a flashback of the witch scuttling around down here like a grotesque spider, her long limbs searching out the rodents and insects who move about unseen in the dark. When she catches one—sometimes the rodents are big, like a rat, whose sizeable body provides quite a feast—the witch sinks her teeth into them and starts to suck at the blood and gnaw at the flesh. When she is sated, she picks the gristle from her teeth, drops the bones and slinks back upstairs, renewed and reenergized.

The old man gags at the sight of this gruesome buffet and drops the bone he holds. Instantly, the reel of images is cut off, but the hideous memories will forever be seared into his mind.

Blood. Life from death. It's how the dark arts have always worked, and it explains how the witch has continued to survive all these years. All these centuries.

A chill sweeps his body. The witch is screaming above him, as if in pain or bitter frustration. Quickly, he lies back down again, not wanting to be caught in any position other than total submission. He is likely to survive longer if she doesn't think he poses any threat.

He hears the door open above, and the witch bounds down the steps, her face contorted with fury. Silas braces for what he thinks will be an all-out assault. Instead, the witch pulls up *short of him and rolls him onto his back. He tries to resist but he can't help staring up at her eyes, the empty eyes of a cadaver, of a body wholly consumed by evil.*

"She is more powerful than I thought," the thing speaks at Silas, a stringy dollop of saliva falling from her lips and onto his chin. "I must have her power. She will make me invincible. My master will be so proud!"

"You'll never have her!" Silas shouts at the witch. "She is stronger than you and she is good! She cannot be taken by the likes of you."

"I can have whatever I want. I just need … a little more strength."

She trails a jagged fingernail along Silas's neck.

"I just need … a little … nourishment."

Abigail Williams pricks Silas's skin with her nail, drawing blood just above his pulsating jugular.

Part Three

"Tis now the very witching time of night, when churchyards yawn and Hell itself breathes out contagion to this world."

William Shakespeare, *Hamlet*

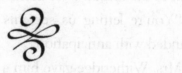

Chapter 25

ABBY AND RYAN followed Mrs. Witheridge into the house.

"It's time we get to work," she said, leading them to the locked door at the end of the hall.

"You're letting us see this room?" Ryan's heart pounded with anticipation.

Mrs. Witheridge gave him a smile. "It's where the magic happens," she told him.

A small silver key appeared in her hand out of

thin air and she pushed it into the lock. Before she opened the door, however, she looked back at Ryan sympathetically.

"I'm sorry I lied to you yesterday," she said.

"What do you mean?"

"I told you everything would be all right. I told you there was nothing to be worried about in these woods. I shouldn't have made light of your very real concerns, but I didn't want to frighten you any more than you already were."

Ryan appreciated the comment. "I understand."

Mrs. Witheridge put a comforting hand on his shoulder. "You'll understand much more very soon."

After glancing at Abby and receiving an affirming nod, she opened the door to her private "study" and led them inside.

Ryan's jaw dropped. The walls were adorned with handcrafted artwork of ancient Celtic signs and symbols. Rugs and mats meant for kneeling covered the floor. Under the window on the opposite wall was a small altar whose surface was covered in candles, spice jars, bowls and pestles. The cramped room was littered with books, some of them opened to pages depicting images of runes and pentacles, others filled with lines of handwritten text in faded ink, like Josiah Martin's journal.

Abby went over to one of the books and read the words aloud: "*Sanguine Luna mortem revolvi novam nativitatem.*" Her pronunciation was a little off, but she recognized some of the root words, even though the verb cases were tricky. She wished she'd paid attention to her father more carefully when he shared his love of Latin with her. He always said the knowledge would come in handy one day.

Today was one of those days.

She gave the translation a little bit more effort, and then she had her ah-ha moment. "*Sanguine Luna mortem revolvi novam nativitatem,*" she repeated. "'The blood moon represents the death of one cycle and the birth of another.'"

"Exactly," said Mrs. Witheridge approvingly as she crossed the room to the altar.

Abby watched in fascination as she lit a stick of incense and three white candles. She recognized the incense at once as Dragon's Blood, a very rare and very powerful tree resin that reinforced spell making. Mrs. Witheridge picked up the stick of incense and waved it around the room. It smelled sweet, spicy and earthy.

"What are you doing?" Ryan asked.

"First, we must cleanse the area of unwanted energies," Mrs. Witheridge intoned.

When she was satisfied the room was properly cleansed, she returned to the altar and picked up a small, slender knife with a black onyx handle. *An athame*, Abby thought. A witch's knife for performing rituals. She watched as Mrs. Witheridge used it to slice into the roots and herbs that she had laying around her table.

Next, Mrs. Witheridge took two sheets of black

felt cloth and started cutting a figure out of them both. They reminded Abby of gingerbread men she'd made in second grade.

"I'm making a poppet," she explained. "It's like a voodoo doll, only this one will be *much* more powerful."

"Do you have everything you need?" Abby said as she watched Mrs. Witheridge deftly stitch the little doll together. Then she added the roots, herbs, crystals and other ingredients she'd prepared into the opening that she left on top.

"Almost. Do you have the potion?"

"Right here." Abby handed the bottle over hesitantly, looking up at Mrs. Witheridge. The old woman's face softened as she understood.

"We haven't talked about your mother yet."

Ryan came over and stood behind Abby.

"She will be okay." Her eyes danced between the two of them. "This potion you found in Silas's cabin ... it's perhaps the most powerful I have ever come

280

across in my life. It can heal or kill, depending on the user's intention. And it takes only a drop." She gazed at it reverentially, holding the bottle in her hand like a precious artifact unearthed from antiquity.

Was that awe or fear that flickered in her eyes? Ryan thought. He wouldn't be surprised if it was both.

Mrs. Witheridge removed the tiny stopper from the bottle and handed it over to Abby. Immediately, a mixture of scents, most of which he couldn't identify, overpowered the incense. He caught floral aromas and woodsy scents, but beneath it all was the heady stench of blood. Ryan brought his hand up to his nose involuntarily. He imagined that walking into a meatpacking plant probably smelled the same, minus the flowers, of course.

Whose blood could it be in that potent mixture? Tituba's herself? Another powerful witch or wizard?

Or something worse?

Mrs. Witheridge carefully tipped the bottle and let one drop fall into the mixture in the poppet. Then she took the stopper back from Abby and sealed the bottle with melted wax before setting it aside.

"Now there is only one thing left to do." She picked up her athame, pressed the tip of the blade to her palm, and uttered these words:

> *"I give my blood to bind you tight,*
> *With my energies I bind you right.*
> *Never walk again in day or night.*
> *Stay in darkness and out of sight.*

As she said the words, three drops of her blood leaked into the unstitched opening of the poppet. When she was finished, she bandaged the cut on her hand and sewed the doll shut.

Ryan swallowed hard and glanced at Abby. Her face had gone white. "Blood magic," Abby whispered, spellbound by what she'd witnessed.

"Don't you *ever* do it," Mrs. Witheridge warned, pointing her finger at both of them. "It's nothing to mess with, at least not until you become experienced practitioners and you've honed your powers."

Mrs. Witheridge noticed the startled look on Abby's face and added kindly, "I know how powerful you are. I just hope you know your own limitations. A witch who deals with forces beyond her capabilities can run into a lot of trouble."

"I understand," she said, and thought, *I wonder if Abigail Williams knew what she was doing when she signed her pact with the devil.* A witch who turns to black magic is reckless and assumes she can handle anything.

Pride is the downfall of the dark witch.

"Now we must energize the poppet." said Mrs. Witheridge, cradling the poppet delicately in her hands.

"How do we do that?" Ryan asked.

"The moon will do it for us." She carried the poppet out of the room. Abby and Ryan followed her outside and watched as she laid it down in a bed of zinnias in her garden. The moon shone radiantly in the sky, but dark clouds were moving in, Ryan noticed. Would it be enough time to energize the poppet and ready it for tomorrow?

"We'll leave it out here overnight," Mrs. Witheridge declared, glancing around at the dark wood. "Tomorrow night we'll perform the sacrament of rights and renew the seal on the witch's evil. We'll have to bury the poppet, however, outside her cabin. It won't be easy. There'll be many dangers. In the meantime …"

A sudden bright light washed through the trees leading up the driveway. A car pulled in and stopped next to them in the driveway. Ryan recognized the man behind the wheel at once. It was Sheriff Chambers. He got out and eyed them all suspiciously before coming around his car to talk to them.

"Strange time to be out doing gardening," he said humorlessly. His face looked long and troubled. The moonlight made the scores of age lines around his eyes and forehead look deep and jagged. When he spoke, his voice sounded hoarse, as though he'd been shouting frequently throughout the night. "I hope I'm not disturbing you," he added.

"Not at all," Mrs. Witheridge said. "Won't you come in? Get a cup of coffee?"

"I won't be staying long," he muttered, shifting from foot to foot.

"Did you find Uncle Silas?" Ryan asked.

"Where's Dad?" Abby asked at the same time.

Sheriff Callahan looked at them each in turn. What they saw in his eyes filled them with dread.

"I guess I'll get right to it," he said, clearing his throat and removing his hat so his restless hands had something to knead. "Your father has disappeared now. He was with our search party scouring Sutter's Hill when one of the deputies reported him missing."

"*What?*" Abby cried.

"No one seems sure when or why he wandered off on his own, but he's gone. No one saw anything. It's like he, well, just disappeared. Like Silas."

Abby felt her anger boil. "My dad wouldn't have just wandered off! Someone must have gotten to him."

"We're looking everywhere, honey. We won't stop until we find him and your uncle." Sheriff Chambers licked his lips and chose his next words carefully. "It's these woods. You can get turned around in them pretty easy, especially at night. And with the animals and other things out there…." His voice trailed off as he gazed warily about him.

"I'm so sorry, Sheriff," said Mrs. Witheridge in a small voice

"Listen," he said to Abby and Ryan. "I don't want to worry you both any more than I already have. I'm sure we'll find them soon. In the meantime, come down to the station first thing in the morning and I'll let you use the phone to call your mother."

"Okay," Ryan said, not knowing what else to say. "Thank you."

"We'll get them back." Sheriff Chambers assured

them as he put his hat back on and turned to leave.

No, you won't, Abby thought. *Abigail Williams won't be caught using normal police procedures, unfortunately.*

And it may already be too late.

Chapter 26

RYAN TOSSED AND turned that night, unable, to get comfortable. He heard Abby groan and whimper several times in her sleep, as though fighting off an attacker. At one point, she even kicked all her bedcovers off.

Despite how his body burned with exhaustion, sleep felt like a remote and unattainable goal. So much was on his mind. He couldn't get Josiah Martin's descriptions of the Salem witch trials out of his head. And then there was Abigail Williams.

Up to now, his only experience with Salem lore had been a movie he'd seen a long time ago. In one scene, the villagers helped drag a screaming woman to the gallows. The frenzied mob jeered at her as they tied the noose around her neck. Families had gathered in the public square and ate picnic lunches while men drank from jugs of moonshine. When the trapdoor sprang and the woman's body dropped, her neck snapped, and the blood-thirsty crowd cheered. Even the children whooped with delight, like they were having the time of their lives on a class field trip.

The curriculum at their school must have been simple: *Turn your back on God and this will happen to you.*

At some point he must have drifted off to sleep, for suddenly he found himself in the middle of a scene just like in the movie—except this time it was Abby's neck inside the noose. The feverish crowd chanted, "Kill the witch!"

Her eyes wide with fright, Abby screamed Ryan's

name over and over until her voice cracked. She fought the men who tied her hands behind her back. The crowd roared with approval when a rag was shoved into her mouth.

Ryan cried Abby's name, but she didn't hear. The faces of the angry townsfolk were full of hate. He tried to shove through the mob to get to her, but they elbowed him back. Helpless, he could do nothing but watch his sister die.

Then, a moment later, the crowd was gone, a jump in time only possible in the sleep realm. Now, the only other person besides himself was Abby, swaying from the rope, staring sightlessly into the dark, her face the pale white of a corpse. A thin ribbon of blood leaked from her blue-tinged lips. He ran up to her and touched her leg, but it was cold as ice. Except for his tears, the only other sound was the creak of the rope.

Then a voice behind him whispered, *"Leave this place at once or this will be your fate. You get no more warnings after this."*

Startled, he spun around, but no one was there.

Then a bolt of white-hot pain tore through his gut, followed by waves of agony, as if a spear impaled his body. He groaned and gasped for air. He could taste his own blood rising in his throat.

"You'll swing like your sister," a hissing voice warned again, *"and your death will be much, much slower."*

"No!" he screamed, his eyes fluttering open. "Don't hurt Abby …!"

Suddenly, he was awake and lying on the cot in Mrs. Witheridge's guest room. Disoriented, he patted his chest and stomach, looking for the gushing wound he thought must be there. There was nothing, nothing but his white T-shirt and clean, white sheets. No blood. He shook his head and fought back the urge to cry. A few tears leaked out anyway, which he quickly brushed aside.

"There's no shame in it," he heard his sister say in the dark. How long had she been awake and watching him struggle in his dream? "We all feel pain," she continued. "Embrace it … pain is our source of power."

"Abby!" he exclaimed. "You're all right!"

"I'm fine. You were just having another nightmare about Abigail Williams. She'd love to get her claws on us, wouldn't she?"

"Yeah, you could say that."

"What did she say to you this time?"

"She threatened to kill us if we didn't leave Black Rock Falls. But you know something? I sensed that she was afraid. Something in her voice…"

"Afraid of us?"

"I don't know … maybe. Maybe she knows we're coming?"

"I'm sure she does." Abby laced her fingers behind her head and stared up at the ceiling. "And when we get there, she'll be ready with the blackest magic we've ever seen."

Chapter 27

IT WAS A fitful night of sleep.

Abby woke early to the sound of rain tapping on the window. She listened to its sad rhythm and thought of her father. The witch had him, she could feel it, and the feelings of desperation and despair crushed her.

Abby couldn't lay there doing nothing anymore. Tucking Josiah Martin's grimoire under her arm, she eased out of bed. Ryan, snoring softly, didn't stir as she tip-toed around his cot and opened the door as quietly as she could. She slipped out into the hallway.

The house was silent. She crept across the hall to Mrs. Witheridge's secret room and slipped a hair pin off the back of her head. Bending it just right, she inserted it into the lock of the door. She'd read about how to pick locks this way but had never tried it before. She hoped the information on the website was correct.

She put her ear up to the knob and listened to the tumblers click and fall into place. Then, withdrawing the pin, she turned the knob. It opened easily, but with a slight squeak. She winced. It sounded like a scream in the heavy stillness of the house. When she was sure no one was aware of her presence, she pushed the door all the way open and stepped inside.

She was not alone.

Chapter 28

THE LAST THING she expected to see was Mrs. Witheridge sitting on a rug in the middle of the room, wearing a long, flowy white robe, her black hair tied up in a ponytail behind her head. On the floor in front of her was a bronze scrying bowl, much like the one Abby had back home. The old woman's eyes were closed like she was meditating. She sat so still Abby wondered if she was even awake.

Worried about disturbing her, she started easing the door shut when Mrs. Witheridge's voice stopped her.

"Come now, dear. Don't be afraid."

Abby froze.

"You have nothing to fear from me." Mrs. Witheridge opened her eyes and locked her gaze on Abby. "After all, what is a witch without her curiosity and her instincts?"

"I didn't mean to pry…"

"I know you didn't. I've been expecting you."

"You were?" Of course, she was. Just as Abby had expected Ryan to grudgingly humor her when she brought her own scrying bowl into his room the other night.

"You're here for the same reason I am," Mrs. Witheridge said. "You want to see if your uncle is all right."

"And Dad," she added.

"The scrying bowl is a witch's eyes," Mrs.

Witheridge beckoned Abby to come into the room and sit down across from her.

"Uncle Silas once told me he can see far and wide, like an eagle soaring," Abby told her.

She smiled. "Yes, like an eagle soaring."

Mrs. Witheridge started waving her hands over the bowl, her fingers twisting in the air as she conjured magic. Abby closed her own eyes, focusing her power as well on the scrying bowl. Mrs. Witheridge started chanting words, a mantra, that urged the spirits to reveal their secrets to her.

Just then, a fluttering began in Abby's stomach, the familiar sensation of dormant magic awakening. It expanded into a full, hot bloom inside her chest, before unfurling its power across her limbs.

Abby envisioned her power emanating from her fingertips like the white beams of flashlights. She aimed these beams of light down to the bowl, willing an image of her uncle to emerge.

"Clear your mind," Mrs. Witheridge ordered.

The room began to grow dark. Shadows lengthened from the corners of the room and glided toward them. Abby felt their presence but didn't dare open her eyes either.

Suddenly this felt like a very bad idea.

The witch's defenses were difficult, if not impossible, to penetrate. Abby was beginning to wish she'd stayed in bed. Sending forth this magical beacon was like shooting a flare off in the dark. The light could attract anything to them …

"Look," Mrs. Witheridge urged her. "Open your eyes. Do you see it?"

She obeyed, but all she saw at first was the water, empty save for the reflections of candlelight. She strained to see beneath the surface. Her vision tunneled until it reached a single point at the bottom of the bowl, and that's when the water's surface began to ripple. Something dark, like a wing, pierced the surface and dove back into the infinite depths just as quickly.

Next, the dark silhouette of a house materialized. Abby recognized it immediately. The cabin from her vision last night. It shimmered in the water and disappeared, replaced by another image. It was a candlelit room inside the cabin, and, crouched in a corner, the figure of a boney woman in tattered black clothing. As their perspective zoomed in closer to the woman, she swiftly turned around and flung something at them!

Abby and Mrs. Witheridge both reacted at the same time. Their hands flew up to protect their faces as water splashed up from the bowl. A raven materialized out of nowhere and circled the room, screeching and cawing, only this time it wasn't an omen as it had been the other night.

It dove straight for their heads several times, its razor-sharp beak tearing at their hands and arms as they tried in vain to wave it away. The raven persisted with brutal efficiency, aiming for cracks in their defenses, stabbing with its slightly hooked beak and ripping gobs of hair off Mrs. Witheridge's head.

Their screaming brought Ryan running into the room, and he immediately tried to help by swatting at the bird. He picked up a candelabra off the altar and swung it at the raven, missing twice but connecting on the third try. The raven dropped to the floor in a heap of bloodied feathers. Ryan tensed, waiting to see what it would do next. When it appeared the bird was too wounded to get up and fly again, he went in for the kill, raising the weapon above his head.

But just before he could bring it down, the bird twitched and rolled over. It started convulsing and flapping its wings in earnest. Its ear-shattering caws started to change. The raven's cries deepened into snorts, snarls, and grunts. To Ryan's utter horror, the raven transformed itself. The feathers dropped off and tufts of sleek gray fur took their place. Its wings morphed into four legs, and its neck and head grew and reformed into a dog's.

No, not a dog.

A wolf.

The beast stood and turned to face Ryan, its hackles raised, and its lips curled back from the sharpest incisors he'd ever seen. In fact, he'd never seen a wolf so *big* before. The ones at the zoo looked like pups in comparison. Its eyes, full of malice, glowed with blood-red fervor.

Ryan slowly lowered the candelabra, realizing he needed to rethink his plan. He wasn't going to be able to beat this creature to death. Any sudden movement on his part would provoke it to attack, and its powerful jaw looked like it could crush steel.

He set the candelabra back down on the altar and raised his hands slowly into the air. The wolf watched his motions warily, but for now held off its attack. It growled again, however, a low deep tone inside its considerable chest. Ryan's own chest felt tight with terror.

He glanced at Abby, who was slowly and silently side-stepping her way to the door. Mrs. Witheridge, on the other hand, stood her ground. In her left hand she held the gleaming athame, business end pointing toward the wolf.

Under her breath she started whispering an incantation. The words were nearly imperceptible, but Ryan picked up *send you back to Hell* more than once. He hoped she could do it.

And send Abigail Williams with it.

But the wolf's ears perked up when it, too, heard the old woman speak. It swung its head around and glared at her, the low growl turning into a full-throated bark. With unbelievable swiftness, it launched itself into the air and knocked Mrs. Witheridge off her feet. The athame flew out of her hand and skittered to a stop at Ryan's feet. He picked it up and charged the wolf. Sensing his attack, it swiped at him with a massive paw, catching him on the jaw. He flew backwards and crashed into a wall, hot pain searing the spot where the wolf had scratched him. Stars exploded before his eyes.

Shaking his head to clear it, he lunged at the wolf again, who now had Mrs. Witheridge pinned to the floor. He saw her trying to hold its head back so its jaws couldn't sink into her throat. She was losing the battle. Its head dipped lower and lower by the second, its front teeth nipping at her neck and drawing blood. Ryan screamed and charged it with the knife held high, and before it could react, he plunged the knife into the base of its neck. Blood spurted around his hand and flowed in red rivulets up his arm. He screamed in pain. The wolf's blood burned like acid. He felt sure he'd carry the scars with him for the rest of his life.

The giant beast gave a final shuddering sigh as its life force ebbed from its body. Ryan rolled it off Mrs. Witheridge and checked her vital signs. The old lady was alive, thank God—or whatever spirits she communed with—but she was badly injured. Though the wolf had missed its mark and left her throat mostly unscathed, its claws had done considerable damage to the rest of her body. Long, oozing scratches ran up and down her legs and stomach, and her robe was soaked in blood.

Together, Abby and Ryan lifted Mrs. Witheridge off the floor and carried her to her bedroom. After setting her in bed, Ryan rushed to get towels, water and bandages. Abby stayed with her and pleaded for her life to the protective spirits watching over her.

Only time would tell if the spirits were merciful.

Chapter 29

THEY TENDED TO Mrs. Witheridge through the rest of the day, waiting for her to wake up.

Several times Ryan wandered around the house with his cell phone in the air, trying to capture bars. He even tried outside, but the woods smothered all cellular communication like a blanket.

He felt like he was trapped in the Stephen King movie *Under the Dome*, where an invisible dome of energy cut the residents of a small town off from the rest of the world. Stranded and alone, he didn't see how they were going to be able to defeat Abigail Williams with Mrs. Witheridge unconscious and the blood moon coming tonight.

At least he was thankful that the rain had stopped. He would take any bit of good news he could find.

While on his third unsuccessful hunt for bars outside, the back-screen door squealed open and Abby strode with purpose out to Mrs. Witheridge's garden. Ryan watched as she grabbed handfuls of purple coneflowers and carried them back inside. He tucked his phone in his pocket and followed.

He found her in the kitchen, standing at the island, grinding the coneflowers and their roots with a pestle. He watched silently as she took the fine dust she'd made and scooped into a small bowl. Next, she turned and searched the cupboards until she found a bottle of whiskey and a piece of cheesecloth. She poured the whiskey slowly into the bowl and then laid the cheesecloth over it, securing it to the bowl with a rubber band. Then she picked the bowl up and started shaking vigorously. Ryan could hear the mixture inside sloshing around.

"What are you—?"

"Making a tincture," she interrupted.

"Oh."

"A potion," she elaborated. "To help heal Mrs. Witheridge's wounds."

Ryan raised an eyebrow.

"Echinacea has healing properties for cuts and burns," she stated matter-of-factly.

"What's the whiskey for then? I don't think Mrs. Witheridge needs to be drinking in her condition right now."

Abby stopped sloshing the bowl around and set it down. "The alcohol breaks down the essential properties of the flower. I should leave it for fourteen days for maximum effect, but there's no time. Get me a cup."

Ryan did as she ordered and plucked a coffee mug off a hook next to Mrs. Witheridge's Keurig.

Gingerly, Abby picked up the bowl and tipped it over upside down, letting the liquid inside drain through the cheesecloth and into the cup. She shook the bowl several times to get every drop, and then set it down in the sink.

Next, Abby picked up the coffee mug and gave it a quick sniff, appearing satisfied with what she'd created. Then she carried the tincture along with a clean towel down the hall to Mrs. Witheridge's bedroom.

"So does she, like, drink that?" Ryan asked awkwardly.

Abby shrugged. "She could, but since she's unconscious, I'm going to spread it on her wounds. It should heal them quickly … I hope."

Ryan watched as she applied the tincture with the cloth over all her scratches and bites. The skin turned redder than before, as if heating up, but when Ryan asked about that, she just told him it was normal. "It's the echinacea beginning to heal her," she said.

When she was finished, they left Mrs. Witheridge's room and let her sleep. Ryan paced the living room restlessly, his eyes never leaving the window. What if the wolves came back? Or the ravens? What if Mrs. Witheridge wasn't well enough before it was time to go to the witch's cabin and perform the sacrament of rites?

Abby sat calmly in one of Mrs. Witheridge's overstuffed armchairs, lost in her own thoughts. She didn't worry like normal people. She could look like she was simply staring blankly into space, but that rapid-fire mind of hers was always churning restlessly with thought.

The hours passed slowly but there still was no sign of Mrs. Witheridge's health improving. Abby checked on her several times.

Finally, as sun sank low and the forest thickened with shadows, Ryan and Abby made the decision.

They had to go alone.

There was no other choice.

Abby brought along the poppet, which thankfully Mrs. Witheridge had brought in sometime during the night before the rain could soak it, and tucked it under her arm along with Josiah Martin's grimoire.

"Grab an umbrella," she told him, "and Tituba's potion." He dutifully complied, searching all the closets until he found an umbrella. He tucked the potion into his pocket.

"Are you sure about this?" he asked as they stepped out into the chill evening air. The clouds were parting, and the moon was beginning its chariot ride across the night sky.

"I'm sure of nothing," she answered him, and added under her breath, "including our safety."

Chapter 30

AS PROMISED, HENRY was hanging around in the woods near Uncle Silas's cabin. All it took was a shout, and he sprung out from behind a maple tree almost like magic.

Or maybe it was magic, Ryan thought. Nothing would surprise him anymore.

"We need your help," Abby told him. Henry looked like he was wearing the same clothes from yesterday. Smelled like it, too. His hair was plastered to the side of his head, like he'd been sleeping all night in the rain.

"For w-what?" he asked, then his gaze dropped to the poppet in Abby's hand. "I-I-I seen one of them before!" he stammered excitedly. "Whatcha gonna do wi-with it?"

"The sacrament of rites," she replied coolly.

Henry's eyes bulged. "You-you can't!"

"Why can't I?"

"You n-need three!" He looked around. "And all I see here is us!"

"How many of us are there?" She glanced at Ryan and gave him a little wink.

"Three." Then a look of shock dawned on his dirt-streaked face. "You can't be … no way! We can't go marchin' up there and—"

"We have to. It's the blood moon tonight." Abby stepped up to him and put a soothing hand on his shoulder. Henry cringed at first but didn't shake her hand away. Ryan was amazed. Over the past twenty-four hours he'd seen his sister show an amazing and uncharacteristic amount of emotion and empathy. He wouldn't say this vacation was good for her, or for any of them, but it certainly was *changing* her. He supposed this trip was changing him as well.

It was time to rethink what was real and possible in this world.

Ryan watched as Henry and his sister locked eyes on each other. They looked like two statues, their features chiseled out of gleaming marble, their expressions ancient and inscrutable.

In the ensuing silence, Ryan could hear his own heart pounding in his ears. Noises in the forest seemed amplified, and time stopped dead in its tracks.

"I understand," she said after a few seconds and dropped her hand away. Those seconds had seemed like an eternity. For a few moments longer, the boy continued to stare at her, his expression a puzzling mixture of awe and something akin to gratitude.

"We should be going," Abby said, glancing up at the sky. "I don't know when exactly the eclipse will start."

"Her cabin is up on Sutter's Hill," Henry reminded them calmly, pushing his way through a thick clump of brambles. The path they followed was almost completely obscured by knotty grass and weeds. In the gathering dark, Ryan didn't know how Henry could see where he was going.

They walked on in silence. Ryan mulled the events over the past forty-eight hours that had brought them to this point where multiple lives, including their own, were on the line. Despite all he'd seen and learned during that time, something he couldn't quite put his finger on nagged him. A question that lingered on the fringe, and that now, finally, stepped into the spotlight.

"Hey, Henry?" Ryan called to the younger boy. "Why hasn't anyone taken it down? You know, the witch's cabin. Why hasn't someone burned it to the ground already and ended all this misery?"

Henry considered the question for a long time before answering. Ryan was beginning to think he didn't hear it or was choosing to ignore him. Then Henry answered, "Because they c-can't. It ain't there."

Ryan stopped in his tracks.

"What do you mean, 'it ain't there'?"

Henry looked back at him, his face whiter than skimmed milk in the darkness.

"I mean, only some folks can see it. The ones with the S-sight."

Abby nodded as if she understood. "Of course. Abigail would have cloaked her home in magic to keep intruders and sightseers away."

Henry added, "And she's got lots of familiars that defend her, wolves and ravens and such."

Ryan didn't say anything. That last statement was obvious. One almost killed Mrs. Witheridge.

As they trudged through the woods, they kept their ears pricked for any signs of wild animals in their vicinity. The forest was unsettlingly quiet, however, as if it were holding its breath and waiting for the big show to begin.

Ryan's curiosity was still unsatisfied. "Why does the moon turn red during an eclipse? It's not like it's really covered in blood or anything."

"Simple," Abby said, her shoes swishing through the grass. "When the moon passes through the earth's shadow, sunlight still strikes its surface, only it has to go through the earth's atmosphere first. That changes the color from white to red."

"Doesn't sound so special to me," Ryan grumbled.

Even in the dark, he could see the frown on his sister's face.

"Any rare astronomical event is going to carry significant mystical power," she informed him.

He should've known better than to argue with her.

They continued picking their way through the woods in silence, keeping close so they wouldn't get separated. The land began to slope up. Their shoes slipped several times on rain-slickened stones and mud.

After several more minutes of hard hiking on

rocky terrain, they reached the peak where the land leveled off and the woods thinned out. The moon, now almost at its highest perch in the sky, beamed down on them full and bright.

Ryan felt the uncomfortable sensation of being watched, and his hands grew cold and clammy. What if the wolves came back? There was no protection in the woods, no trees around that they could climb fast enough to escape. Whenever a twig snapped, he whipped around, expecting to find something lurking in the shadows, but nobody was there. He noticed the birds had stopped singing, as though afraid of disturbing the uneasy peace on the hill.

Although the skeptical part of him held out hope that he'd find a logical explanation for the horrors he'd witnessed, that voice was growing more and more resigned with each step. He'd seen too much, learned too much, to really believe that all this was simply a delusion.

Abigail Williams was waiting somewhere up ahead,

biding her time, probably laughing at the arrogance of three kids coming to confront her.

Henry and Abby halted so abruptly he almost ran into them.

"What are you guys doing?" He squinted ahead but saw nothing unusual but a clearing in the middle of a ring of trees. "Why'd you stop?"

"D-don't you see it?" Henry asked.

Ryan shook his head. "What am I looking at?"

Abby whispered to Henry, "He doesn't have the Sight yet."

"Can you give it to him?"

Abby looked over her shoulder at her brother, twirling a lock of her hair around her finger. "I don't know if he's ready. He's a bit of a project."

Ryan stomped ahead and spread his arm apart. "What is so fascinating about a bunch of grass?" he said. "Shouldn't we be trying to find the cabin?"

"Wow," Henry said.

Abby nodded. "He only looks with his eyes." Her

new friend nodded matter-of-factly, as though Ryan were a specimen they were studying in a lab. "He doesn't yet utilize all of his other senses," she added.

She came forward and gently touched her brother's shoulder. "Be calm," she told him in a soothing voice. "Remember what I told you about Uncle Silas? How he helped me see the world in a new way?"

"In the woods," Ryan replied slowly. "The butterflies and stuff."

"Yes, the butterflies. I can show you how to tap into your magic, but you have to have an open heart. And you have to trust me."

A cold shiver rippled through his body. When she talked like this, it usually creeped him out—but this time it was different. He knew Abby better now than he did before. She was more than a quirky girl with autism. Maybe it wasn't truly autism in the first place but something much more mysterious and unfathomable. Maybe it was her gift, the depths of which even she probably hadn't discovered yet, that made her seem so odd next to everybody else.

So, of course, he'd trust her. He'd let her lead him this far, hadn't he? There was no sense in stopping now.

Besides, the lives of his father, uncle, and even his mother were at stake.

She read all this in his mind with her accustomed ease and placed her hand over his heart. "Are you ready?"

"I guess so." He looked down at her hand and the odd warmth emanating from her fingers.

"Close your eyes."

Summoning his courage, he listened to her rhythmic voice describe inner channels in his mind filled with a white light, a warren of power underlying all living things. How he could tap into it if he guided his thoughts to unlock the right doors. It was about *will* and determination. It was about silencing self-doubt and skepticism. It was about seeing what truly *was*, rather than looking at what you expect to see.

"You need to *believe* in yourself, Ryan," she said, her voice rising. "Believe in your power!"

Ryan did. He believed. He believed in everything he'd seen the past two days, he believed in his sister and her abilities, and he believed the witch could be overcome. And, above all, he believed in the unseeable, the unknowable, and the world beyond his own senses. And the power that resided in himself.

That last thought surprised him, but there it was. Total honesty. Truly, it felt like a lid lifted and the pent-up steam of so much negativity had been released from his soul.

He was *positive* they would leave this damnable place tonight with Uncle Silas and their father.

Or die trying.

When she finished speaking, Ryan felt wholly different: light-headed and shaky in the knees, and somewhat removed from himself, as though his soul was having an out-of-body experience without his permission. He actually enjoyed the pleasant sensation of lightness and effervescence fizzing in every cell of his body.

"Open your eyes now," she whispered.

He did … and, oh, how the world had changed! The trees, the sky, the grass and flowers … even in the moonlight, he saw their contrasting colors, their delicate yet wondrous structures. Their individual fragrances were sharper than he'd ever experienced before, and the sounds of every restless movement in the forest was crystal clear. He felt like a part of it all, a vital piece of nature—not a link in a chain or a thread in a fabric, but an inextricable element in the essence of *everything*.

Abby smiled as she watched her brother experience all the new sensations. "Life moves through you and *with* you," she said. "The inner channels of your mind are filled with light, a source of power underlying all living things."

Ryan opened his mouth to say something, but as

quickly as he'd thought the words, they were gone. He wasn't sure what words he could possibly say to describe what he was feeling.

"Now turn around and see," she told him.

He did.

A small cabin, about half the size of their uncle's and shaped like a lumpish brown mushroom, sagged miserably in the middle of the clearing...the clearing that had moments ago been empty.

He gasped. "How did that get there?"

"It's always been there, hidden by magic," Abby told him. "You just had to take your blindfold off."

"I toldja I knew w-where the cabin was!" Henry exclaimed proudly.

"I never said you were lying," Ryan said. *I just thought you were a little off.* But he kept that little piece of information to himself, especially since he felt guilty now for thinking it.

They picked their way along the edge of the woods like they were approaching a wounded animal, careful not to get too close. Ryan recognized the architecture as being from the early colonial period, based on a project he'd done in the eighth grade. The rough-hewn logs stacked horizontally and interlocked at the ends with notches to form the basic square of the house itself. There was a crumbling chimney made of mud and stone, and a small door cut into the side of the cabin that faced them. A few tiny openings in the wooden walls served as windows.

The cabin appeared to be deserted. It sat there in its own little nest of shadows like an abandoned egg laid by some gigantic foul creature.

"It's empty," Ryan said.

"No, it isn't," Abby corrected him, pointing to one of the cabin windows. "Listen."

Inside the darkened cabin, something stirred. Footsteps scraped a wooden floor, followed by the sound of wings slicing the night air.

"Take this." Abby shoved the poppet into Ryan's arms. "Get ready."

"For what?" he asked.

"I'll tell you where to bury it, then I'll start saying the incantation."

An eerie howl echoed through the woods.

"H-hurry," stammered Henry. He pointed to the moon. "I-it's starting!"

Abby and Ryan gazed up at the full moon. A tiny sliver of it was already dipped in blood.

Chapter 31

"WE NEED TO move fast," Abby said. "Ryan, start digging the hole right here."

She pointed to a mossy patch of ground a few yards into the clearing

"Okay." He started walking to the spot she indicated and stopped. He spun around and faced her.

"Abs, I didn't bring a shovel!"

The horror-stricken look on her face said it all. How could they have forgotten such a basic and essential thing?

Now they were in trouble.

"Use your hands!" she cried, glancing up at the moon. "We don't have time to argue!"

"G-guys, I think I see something moving in the c-cabin..."

Ryan ignored Henry and dropped to his knees. Luckily, the rain from earlier in the day made the ground soft. He was able to easily scoop big clumps of damp soil out with his hands.

"How deep do I have to go?" he asked.

Abby didn't answer. She had the grimoire open and was beginning to recite the incantation.

Ryan returned to his work of burying the poppet when Henry suddenly let out a scream. A raven shot out of the window like a bullet, racing right for Ryan's head. He ducked just in time to avoid the collision, but when he looked to see where it had gone, he found Henry slumped over on the ground, grabbing his chest.

"What was … that?" He coughed, and Ryan thought he saw blood. The raven lay sprawled on the ground at his feet, flipping over and over as if trying to regain its senses. Angry, Ryan rushed over and stomped on the bird, hearing the satisfying crunch of its bones under his sneaker.

"Are you all right, Henry?" he asked the boy who winced in pain as he tried to sit up on the grass.

"I think so." Then his eyes widened in alarm. "Look out!"

The cabin disgorged a swarm of blackbirds. Ravens shot from the chimney and exploded out the windows, rising into the air in a single black cloud, blotting out the moon. The paper-shredding sound of their wings echoed through the woods, and their piercing *caws* made an ear-splitting din.

"Ryan!" Abby shrieked. "Bury the poppet now!"

But Ryan couldn't move. His feet wouldn't obey the command from his horror-struck brain. He stood rooted to the spot, gawping up at the writhing mass of frenzied birds.

"They're going to at—"

Before he could get the rest of his sentence out, the ravens formed a massive and terrifying arrow in the sky and shot themselves straight at Ryan.

"Run!" Ryan grabbed Abby and pushed her toward the woods. "Run and hide. I'll get Henry," and he reached out to scoop Henry off the ground.

"I can't make it!" Henry brushed his hand away. "Go! Leave me!"

"We're not going without you!"

He tried to help Henry up, but it was too late. The ravens, sensing the weak and wounded, swarmed around the boy, pecking and ripping at his skin like carrion left behind for the taking. Ryan kicked and flailed at the birds, sometimes crushing one's beak or breaking another one's neck, but they were too possessed by a need for murder. They continued to swarm Henry until he slumped over onto the ground, lifeless.

Abby came forward to help Henry.

"Abby, don't!" Ryan caught his screaming sister and dragged her away to the safety of the woods, meager and insufficient as that safety was.

"They're killing him!" she shrieked.

"There's nothing we can do; there's too many of them!" Ryan started running, dragging his sister by the hand behind him.

"Henry!" she cried once more, but the boy who used to be Henry Alden lay in a heap of bloody clothes, his empty eyes staring blankly at them.

"I'm so sorry, Abs," Ryan panted, leading them back down the hill as fast as he could go. His sister gave up any attempt to resist and ran with him, apparently realizing it was the only choice.

The plan ruined, they reached the same dark conclusion together: Not only did they get a friend killed, but the spell over Abigail Williams would be broken. The witch would be free to walk the earth again, casting her long shadow of vengeance over everyone responsible for her centuries-long imprisonment.

He felt Abby's fingernails dig into his hand. "We have to go back, Ryan! We need to finish what we started, before it's too late!"

"What are you talking about?" He couldn't believe what she was saying. They'd be killed in seconds. There were too many ravens to fight off, and they'd never get back to the cabin in time.

When he looked up, he saw the moon was already half red; the eclipse was upon them, and with each passing second, the witch's powers would only intensify. He wouldn't do it. He swore to his parents that he'd protect his sister at all costs. He'd die fighting to keep her alive. If it came to it, he'd throw his body over hers and let the crows feast on him to their hearts' content. They'd satiate their hunger eventually and return to whatever blasphemous nesting site they came from, wouldn't they?

Wouldn't they?

Besides, there was his mother to think about. She was dying, and she needed the potion Ryan carried in his pocket. Perhaps they could return to deal with Abigail Williams later.

Abby must have sensed his doubt and confusion because she stopped running. "We can't run anymore, Ryan." Her stare burned a hole straight through him. "Don't be afraid. Remember what I told you earlier."

They both heard a soft, sinister laugh in their ears. It didn't sound like it came *from* the forest so much as the forest itself was mocking them.

They turned and faced the ravens that filled the sky like an impenetrable black curtain, blocking the blood-stained moon and casting a deep black shadow over them. Ryan could hear the clicks and scrapes of their beaks and the wave-like rhythm of their onrushing wings.

What was it that Abby had said earlier? *Inner channels of his mind filled with white light. A source of power underlying all living things.*

All he had to do was clear his mind of doubt and *believe* in his own power.

He held his hands up in front of him, palms open, arms outstretched. He envisioned a tiny trapdoor in the basement of his mind springing open, releasing a brilliant white light that came pouring out, momentarily blinding him and bathing his whole body in warmth.

He felt its recoil through his arms and legs. Every blood vessel of his body was on fire. He thought of himself as a glowing battery capable of charging a house, a town ... even a city.

The brilliance momentarily baffled the ravens. They pulled up and stopped mid-air, spinning in haphazard circles, some even crashing into trees and falling to their deaths on the forest floor. They cawed and complained about the bright light that burned their coal-black eyes. Their rage, and the witch's behind it, was a force that pushed against his own with a hunger that would stop at nothing to get to him. But he pushed back, fearless, every muscle in his body stretched to the breaking point. Out of the corner of his eye he noticed he wasn't alone in the fight; Abby glowed like an overheated bulb too, her power merging with his own.

Blinded by the intensity of the light, the ravens continued crashing into trees and each other, breaking limbs in gruesome fashion, and plummeting to the ground at their feet. It rained death from the sky for another minute before the pressure let up and the last of the ravens, apparently desperate to live, fluttered back into the woods. When the sound of their complaints faded, the woods were still and silent again. The moon shone down on them again, fully wearing its red cloak this time.

The blood pounded in Ryan's ears.

They were too late.

"Ryyyaaann," hissed a voice from somewhere to his right. He peered into the woods but saw nothing.

"Aaabbyyy."

Now the voice came from their left. The witch was toying with them now.

Ryan tried to slow his breathing down and gather his wits, but he was exhausted from fighting off the ravens and just wanted to rest. The witch cackled behind them. They spun around.

Up the path in the woods walked Abigail Williams, her soiled bare feet poking out from under the bottom of a long and tattered black frock. Her eyes glowed a shade of scarlet deeper than the moon's, no doubt lit by the furnace of evil burning in her soul. To Ryan's horror, he noticed the witch's physical body already in a state of semi-decomposition. The old woman's joints creaked and popped as her legs carried her in a series of jerky, halting movements. The seam of her mouth cracked into an appalling rictus stuffed with yellow rotting teeth. From the pit of her throat emerged a long, pink tongue, wagging between her pustuled lips like a venomous snake probing the air.

And tasting their fear.

"What did you do?" the witch taunted, her eyes flicking between the both of them. His sister trembled and stepped behind Ryan.

Abigail Williams looked thoughtful as she studied Abby for a moment. "The girl who shares my name," she said with interest. "I believe I will kill you first. Then I will honor the death of a witch as fine as yourself by joining your powers with mine."

Next her eyes flicked to Ryan's, and she scowled. A blade of horror stabbed his chest. "Then I will kill your hero and roast him over an open pit. *Slowly*. I wouldn't want to spoil the meat."

The witch took another awkward step toward them, waving her arms in the air before her. A hot, swirling wind started at the ground around their feet and worked its way up, kicking up dirt and leaves until they were almost blinded by the cyclone.

What happened next was a blur. Ryan felt the bindings of black magic tightening around his legs, but before they could restrain him fully, he acted. He shouted, dropped his shoulder, and in three large strides struck the witch full force in the chest. She gave out a surprised cry and stumbled backward onto the ground, with Ryan landing on top of her. It felt like falling onto a pile of sharp twigs and sticks. He heard snapping and crunching and knew he'd broken several of her ribs. Abigail Williams screamed in pain and flung him off her with incredible and unexpected strength.

She tried to gain her feet, but her rickety legs wobbled under her and she fell once again. Ryan saw his chance. He charged ahead again and tackled her once more to the ground, pinning her down with his legs. He dug around in his jeans for the potion but came up empty. Frantic, he looked around for it. It must have fallen out of his pocket! And that's when he saw Abby, holding something in her hand. The bottle. He called for it and she tossed it to him. He caught it in one hand, and with the other uncorked the top…

This potion you found in Silas's cabin ... it can heal or kill, depending on the user's intention. And it takes only a drop.

...and poured several drops into her eyes and mouth. The witch let out a roar that pierced his eardrums. The liquid scorched her eyes, burned them shut, and did the same to her throat. Sores and pustules started to ooze; the stink made him gag. He rolled off of Abigail Williams and went over to stand with Abby. They watched the witch writhe in torment, claw the air, and gurgle curses from deep within her ruined throat.

Ryan heard a chant coming from somewhere, and it took him a moment to realize that Abby was casting a spell.

> *Your time on earth has come and gone;*
> *we send you to your dusty grave*
> *Leave this world and do not return;*
> *The souls you cursed have now been saved.*

Abigail Williams was starting to fade. Her body shivered with spasms as curls of smoke rose up from her tattered frock. Her skin sagged and peeled, melting off her bones like candle wax. The outline of her skull protruded from behind her cheekbones and jaw, and before their very eyes, Abigail Williams became a sickly sack of bones, muttering and twitching on the wet grass. A gurgle escaped her throat—one last curse, one last agonized protest against the world she hated—and then the witch responsible for Salem's horror long ago fell silent.

Abby stopped chanting.

"It's over," she declared, turning her back on the witch. "Let's go rescue Dad and Uncle Silas."

Chapter 32

T HE SILENCE OF the night closed in around
them like a vast tomb as they ran back down the
path to the cabin. There was no sign of the ravens
from earlier—nor, to Ryan's relief, of the wolves.

When they reached the cabin, they found the door
was locked, but with two powerful kicks, Ryan was
able to break it in.

The tiny cabin was a mess. A small cooking fire
burned in the hearth and a kettle of foul-smelling

liquid boiled over it. The skeletons of numerous animals lay about, as well as knives, plants, roots and herbs. The place looked like a storm had struck it. Of course, home décor would have been low on Abigail Williams' list of priorities.

"Why are you smiling?" Abby asked. "We don't even know if Dad and Uncle Silas are alive!"

Ryan shook his head. "You wouldn't understand."

Or would she?

They walked around in the cabin, looking for a hiding place where the men might have been stashed, when Abby spotted the trap door.

"Under the floor!" she exclaimed. They grasped the small metal ring that served as a handle and yanked the door up. A breath of cool, dank air rose from the hole in the floor.

"Uncle Silas?" Abby called. "Dad?"

"Down here!" croaked their uncle's voice.

It was Abby's turn this time to break into a wide grin of triumph. "We found them," she said though joyful tears.

Ryan gave his sister's shoulders a squeeze and kissed the top of her head. "No, *you* found them."

Chapter 33

"WE'LL RETURN IN a few days for the funeral," said their father the next morning as he loaded the last suitcase into the car. He shook Uncle Silas's hand and gave Mrs. Witheridge a hug. "I'm sorry things turned out the way they did."

They all felt sorry for poor Henry. His father broke down in tears when Ryan and his dad brought the body to him. Arrangements for services were made quickly, and the sheriff's office launched an investigation into the death. Police officers were at Mrs. Witheridge's cottage before the sun was even up, and a thousand questions were asked and answered. But, oddly, it was the private face-to-face that Sheriff Chambers had with Uncle Silas that seemed to resolve the matter quickly. All Uncle Silas would say of the words exchanged between the two long-time friends were, "He sees it now. He knew the reckoning was coming sooner or later."

And just like that, Ryan and his family were free to go.

Remarkably, Ryan didn't feel like going home yet. He wanted to stay and talk to his uncle about all the questions piling up in his mind about who he was, his family history, and especially his newfound power.

Abby squeezed his hand. As usual, she was glued to his side, staring stoically at Uncle Silas and Mrs. Witheridge. Her feelings were back to being as incomprehensible as ever, though Ryan knew she wasn't the same Abigail Rebecca Martin who visited

Black Rock Falls three days ago.

This new girl would be even more interesting.

Mrs. Witheridge came over and gave them both a hug. Ryan was surprised at how quickly the echinacea tincture worked on her wounds. You would have never known how close she came to being mauled by a hellish wolf and bleeding to death.

"You take care, dear," she whispered to Abby, and gave her a warm smile. "We'll talk some more when you come back."

Uncle Silas clapped Ryan on the back. Despite everything he'd been through, the old man was just as Ryan remembered: tall, wiry, and strong, with an easy smile and infectious laugh. His handshake felt like vice grips around Ryan's hand, and his blue eyes, though sunken and filled with exhaustion, were still as sharp as ever.

"Thank you," he said to his nephew sincerely. "We'll catch up on that fishing, I promise. It'll give us a chance to talk."

"I'd like that," Ryan said, beaming.

Their father ushered them into the car and said his final farewells. The engine roared to life, and he waved once last time at Silas.

"Don't do anything I wouldn't do," he said, waving out the window.

"Don't worry," he answered with a hearty laugh. "I already did!"

After they were out of the woods and on the open highway, Ryan announced he had bars and would try to call their mother. Their house phone rang six times before going to the answering machine. Her cell phone also went straight to voice mail.

"Try again," Dad said, frowning. "They must be home. Where else would they be?"

Nobody wanted to think about the answer to that question.

Ryan started calling his aunt Kim when he noticed his text messages. Twenty-eight! He'd been out of range for so long that they'd been piling up. He opened the message app and read through the list of senders. There were five from Aunt Kim, along with three voice mails. There were probably even more on their dad's phone. Ryan read the most recent text message, sent last night around seven o'clock: Taking your mother to the hospital now. Not good. CALL ME!!!

"Did you get through to anybody?" Dad asked tersely, pushing the accelerator a little harder.

"Yes," Ryan said, emotion choking his voice. "We need to hurry!"

Chapter 34

WHEN THEY ARRIVED at the hospital, a nurse at the front desk told them that their mother was on the seventh floor of the cancer wing, room 780. Clutching Abby's hand, Ryan followed their dad as he walked briskly to the elevators. Abby legs were stiff as a board; her breath quickened as the elevator took them up to her floor. When her hand started to tremble, Ryan gave it a reassuring squeeze. He was scared, too—terrified, really—more than he'd been around the witch.

"Do you have it?" she whispered to him.

He patted the side of his cargo shorts. Tituba's tincture lay at the bottom of his pocket. He gave Abby a nod, and she visibly relaxed.

A few minutes later, they opened the door to their mother's room and stepped inside. Ryan's heart sank. She was propped up on pillows, sleeping heavily, her chest shuddering with labored breaths. Her face was gaunt, her eyes hollowed out and filled with purple shadows. It looked like at least ten more pounds had melted off her body in just the last few days. He could see the shape of her skull underneath her skin, like her face was a mask barely disguising death. A deep, profound sadness welled up in him, and he couldn't hold back his tears any longer.

He rushed to the bed and hugged her. She stirred slightly, and her eyes fluttered open for a moment like she was trying to clear her foggy mind. His father and Abby held back a moment, giving him his time, and then they too approached the bed and stood by their mother. A doctor came into the room and gave an update on her prognosis to their father. They spoke in low tones, but Ryan heard pieces, and the pieces he heard depressed him further.

Cancer metastasizing.

Now in her kidneys, intestines, liver and lungs.

Pain under control.

Chemotherapy not an option.

Surgery not an option.

Days, not months.

Days.

When the doctor was finished giving his gloomy assessment of her condition, he excused himself quietly and left the room.

Her brow furrowing with concern, Abby stared at their mother. He knew his sister's heart must be breaking and her emotions overwhelming her. He didn't know how she could lock her feelings away so tightly. He felt like a piece of crystal that could shatter into a million pieces at the slightest touch. By contrast, Abby seemed resolved and defiant.

And strong.

Finally, she tore her gaze away from their mother and looked at him.

Give me the potion and leave me alone with her.

Ryan heard her request, a simple thought passing breezily through his mind.

He surreptitiously passed the bottle to Abby and then turned to their father.

"Dad?"

"What is it, Ryan?" he asked.

"I think Abby may need some time to process, you know?" He tried to think of what else to say that would persuade his father to leave them alone. "I think maybe we should leave her alone and let her talk to Mom?"

Their father studied Abby for a second. "Would you like to be alone with her for a few minutes?" he asked gently.

Abby nodded slightly.

"Okay." He kissed her on the top of her head. "I'll be right outside."

"I'll catch up in a minute," Ryan told him as he slipped out the door quietly.

"Okay, son."

He turned back to his sister and watched anxiously as she removed the tincture from her jacket pocket. Without taking her eyes off her mother, Abby uncorked the bottle. Then she carefully poured a single drop of the potion into the cup of water on the tray next to the bed.

"She needs to drink this now," Abby said, and instantly Ryan leapt into action. He came around to the other side of the bed and shook his mother's shoulders gently.

"Wake up, Mom. You have to wake up." She moaned groggily and tried to open her eyes. Gingerly, he held her head up as Abby brought the cup to her lips.

At first a little liquid dribbled down her chin, but then the muscular reflexes took over and she began to drink some of the water. At first just a few sips, then a full swallow. He gently laid his mother's head back on the pillow and glanced worriedly at the door.

If they were caught …

"We won't be," Abby said confidently, startling him. "C'mon. We need to let her rest."

"Will the medicine…?"

"Yes. The magic is pure and strong."

Ryan felt a huge weight lift off his shoulders.

The magic is in the box.

Yes, it was. Waiting for her all this time.

Chapter 35

RYAN STOOD AT the swimming pool's edge,
staring down at the crystalline water, preparing to
jump. Abby stood beside him, watching. Only
she wasn't watching him, Ryan realized. She was
staring at their mother, who shouted words of
encouragement and laughed easily and good-
naturedly, as though the events of the past few weeks
had ever happened. She wore her favorite wide-
brimmed summer hat and oversized sunglasses. She

354

was looking better each day, healthier. Her skin was no longer a cadaverous gray, and she was putting on weight again. Her strength, along with her spirit, had returned as well.

In just two short weeks after taking the potion, the cancer had miraculously gone into remission. All the doctors were stunned. No one had an explanation.

Abby and Ryan understood perfectly well what happened, however, and so did their mother, who told them last night, "Our little secret. No one else needs to know. Who'd believe us anyway?"

Ryan marveled at the miracle of her quick recovery several times in private to Abby, but she appeared almost indifferent to it. "The wonders of modern science can't hold a candle to traditional witchcraft," she pronounced one day, and then turned around and walked away without another word on the matter. In some ways, she was back to her old self; in others, she was an entirely different person. Happy might be a good word to describe her now, but he didn't think it was quite right. *Satisfied* seemed closer to the truth. As if all the pieces of her world had been put back together in the right order.

"Do a cannonball and splash your mother!" Dad shouted, and Ryan was about to do just that when Abby walked suddenly away from him and approached their parents.

"What is it, honey?" Mom asked.

Abby blinked and stared at her.

"What's wrong?"

"Why did you do it?" she finally asked.

"Do what?"

"Why did you name me after *her*?"

Their mother and father exchanged a knowing glance, as though they'd been expecting this question for a while now. Mom reached out and embraced her, and said loud enough for Ryan to hear, "We didn't name you after her. We named you Abigail because the name means 'a father's joy' in Hebrew."

"That's right," said Dad. "You and Ryan are more

precious to us than anything else in the world. Abigail Williams doesn't get to own the name. You're my little girl, and that's all that matters."

Abby considered this for a moment, and then she broke out in a broad grin.

"I love you," she said, hugging both her mother and father.

"Hey," Ryan called to his sister once all the hugging was done. "You ready to do this or what?"

Abby trotted over to the pool to join him.

"You don't have to jump in if you don't want to," he murmured. "You could always go to the library and find a book on mummies or something."

Abby considered the idea. "No. Last time I looked they were all checked out."

Ryan grinned.

"Besides, there'll be time for reading later," she said, and she dove into the water! Ryan followed behind her, and they splashed and played in the pool for the first time since either of them could remember.

ACKNOWLEDGEMENTS

There is an old expression—many hands make light work. For authors, many eyes make better writing. Thank you to the following people for taking the time to give my novel a close read:

Michael Sisson, English teacher extraordinaire, for all the edits and insights you shared. Sarah Goodman-Brown and Julie Lawrence for the suggestions you offered to make the story stronger. To SheaLeigh Brown for taking the time out of your busy life as a teenager to read my manuscript and share your thoughts. Finally, a special thank you to my wife, Jennifer, and my dad, Gary, for their love, support, and constructive criticism of my book.

Without all of you, *Curse of the Witch* might have never made it out of the dark.

If you enjoyed *Curse of the Witch*,

you might also like...

A Night Long Ago ...
Halloween, 1892

It was a house with a cold heart and a long memory. And a house of many doors, with many rooms and many passageways in which to slip unseen through the dark.

Candles winked and flickered in the windows of the mansion called Blystone Manor. Shadows grew and stretched like serpents in the moonlight. The wind breathed cold and stirred the forest, waving the trees back and forth like hands beckoning the people to come.

And the people came.

They came from nearby towns and villages, in wagons and carriages and on foot. They came with family and friends. They came to laugh, to scream, to delight in the horrors prepared for them by the owner of the mansion, James W. Blystone. Every dimly lit

1

room and corridor of the mansion would be haunted this evening. And those souls brave enough to wander the mansion and search out its secrets would not be disappointed.

Most of all, they came for the masquerade party. Laughter and music flooded the Grand Ballroom. Werewolves spun mummies, court jesters swayed cheek to cheek with Egyptian princesses, and maidens lunged with Roman generals. The Grand Ballroom was decorated in lavish style. Tapestries hung on the walls. Curtains of dark purple silk swooped across windows. The beeswax-polished floor gleamed under a massive golden chandelier. In the air lingered the sweet aromas of meats, breads, cakes, and pies, all laid out on huge banquet tables. The feasting went on all evening until the strings of the orchestra fell silent.

Then all eyes turned to the grandfather clock in the corner. No one moved or talked or ate or drank. Even the children fell silent with enchantment, listening to the final seconds tick away before the grandfather clock announced the stroke of midnight.

The end of moments.

The witching hour.

"Unmask!"

The first cry went up and was soon followed by another. People cheered and shouted and tore their masks off, flinging them into the air like a swarm of bats.

Amid the celebration, a small figure drifted unnoticed through the crowd. She made its way swiftly to the banquet tables, hesitating before picking up a heavy, silver candelabrum. As the crowd lost itself in the jubilant moment of unmasking and called for the tired orchestra to strike up another tune, the girl suddenly pitched forward and lost her grip on the candelabrum, which slipped from her hand.

The dozen lit candles struck the floor and caught fire to the nearest tapestry. Moments later a blaze spread up to the ceiling and across the walls. One scream followed another as the crowd pushed and shoved each other out of the way, in a mad frenzy to escape.

The girl tried to slip away unseen down the spiraling staircase but was caught in the flood of servants coming up to put out the fire. Crushed between the crowd stampeding down and the one coming up, her pleas for help were smothered in the confusion. As smoke curled thick and black around her, she passed out, and awoke much later to find things really hadn't changed much at all.

The house was still there. Cold and dark as ever.

Silent as a grave.

CHAPTER ONE
Tuesday, October 13, 2005
Day 1

Eyes.

They watched Seth. From every dark corner and through the tiniest cracks in the walls. Eyes followed Seth in every room of the house, but especially *his* room, as if someone or something was hunting him.

Eyes made his skin crawl. He always wondered about that. How could skin crawl? He didn't know, but when he stood alone in the middle of his bedroom, on the first night in his new house, he understood.

Your skin could very easily crawl.

Especially when you were being watched.

Seth looked around his new room. His messy new room. Boxes stacked up all around the floor. Magazines, books, and games spilling around his bed. The bedroom was

5

large, twice as big as his old one back in Ohio, with a walk-in closet, antique writing desk, and a wicker rocking chair sitting in the corner next to his bed.

He liked his room, though he hated the house. He didn't want to be here. Blystone Manor was too big, for one thing. Too many rooms, hallways, staircases, and passageways. Too much quiet. Too much dust. Too many ageless portraits of famous people who once lived in Blystone. The house was very old.

Too much time.

And the air in the mansion was gloomy and cold, as if a fog bank hovered over all the rooms. Including his own.

Too depressing.

This would be a perfect house to film a horror movie in, Seth thought. He could be the star. The story would be about a boy who was dragged halfway across the country, told he would never see his friends or school again, and forced to live in a house haunted by unfriendly spirits who wanted him out.

This mansion, or something unseen in it, kept its eyes on Seth like a tom cat stalking a rat. He felt afraid to go into certain places.

But what could be dangerous about Blystone Manor?

Seth didn't know.

And didn't want to find out.

A few minutes later his mother came in to check on him and say good-night. She was dressed in the same clothes she wore all day— jeans and a blue Old Navy sweatshirt. Her bloodshot eyes sagged with exhaustion.

"So do you still think the house is haunted?" she asked.

Seth shrugged. Earlier in the day when they'd first arrived at the house, he told his mother he felt uncomfortable. He knew he sounded paranoid, but he confessed to feeling like someone or something was following him around the mansion.

"I don't know," he admitted. "Maybe it's my imagination."

"New house, new school. A brand-new life." His mother smiled reassuringly. "It's a lot for a kid to take in."

Seth grinned. He was already in bed, listening to music, the volume turned down. The tiny lamp next to his bed burned dimly. He appreciated his mother trying to cheer him up, though it wasn't working entirely. He still felt *strange*.

"I thought I heard voices earlier," he said after a long pause. He stared at his sheets, afraid of what he might see in his mother's face. A disappointed look, maybe? Or a look that told Seth he was going crazy.

"I think you're just homesick," his mother said, patting his shoulder. She added, "You like your room, don't you?"

"Yes," he said, though the closet freaked him out a little. So big. It was almost another room itself. Anything could be hiding in there.

"Your father and I want you to be happy here," his mother continued. "When he found out he was inheriting this house from his uncle, he was so excited. This place is" –she searched for the right word— "amazing." She raised her hands in the air like a game show hostess showing off a new prize. "Who would have ever thought that the Porters would live like royalty?"

"Okay, Mom." Seth grinned. He'd try his best to like the mansion. If not for himself then for his parents. He knew they loved him and wouldn't have moved him to a place that would hurt him. Would they?

When she left the room and turned off the light, he closed his eyes and sighed. He tried to push it from his mind that his tiny house in Ohio was now standing empty, lonely, like a lost pet. How he wanted to go back and visit! But he had to forget ... *forget*. He wiped the memories of home away and sank into the dark waters of sleep.

9 780578 632285